SIONA'S
TALE

SIONA'S TALE

Barbara A. Liepe

ILLUSTRATIONS BY MADDIE KATHLEEN

SIONA'S TALE

iUniverse books may be ordered through booksellers or by contacting:

iUniverse
1663 Liberty Drive
Bloomington, IN 47403
www.iuniverse.com
1-800-Authors (1-800-288-4677)

ISBN: 978-1-5320-3896-9 (sc)
ISBN: 978-1-5320-3895-2 (e)

Library of Congress Control Number: 2017918912

Print information available on the last page.

iUniverse rev. date: 02/21/2018

To the memory of my mother and father

Because of you my heart leapt too.
Because of you I breathed.

From the new comes the old.
From the old comes the new.

Author's Note

WHEN WAS THE LAST TIME you read a book with marine invertebrates as the key literary characters? And I'm not talking about a textbook with bunches of marine invertebrates as subjects for study, like *Aplysia californica* as a model organism for learning and memory or *Ciona intestinalis* as a model for whole-genome analysis. And don't even think about a sponge as an engineering guide to fiber optics or as the inspiration for the generation of complex molecules using palladium-catalyzed cross-coupling. Marine invertebrates largely have been underrepresented in literature. This book is an attempt to cast our spineless cousins in key roles.

Siona's Tale is a work of fiction. It is fictionally factual and factually fictitious, a scientific fantasy. The characters and creatures in this story are imaginary. Lobsterlike Cambrian creatures absolutely cannot write the alphabet with their claws. Sea stars, hares, spiders, shrimps, and clams as we know them today likely did not exist during the Cambrian explosion, and flagella large enough to whip even a tiny larva senseless are impossible. But the narrative is intended to touch upon some basic concepts in science: evolution, the nature and perception of light and color, DNA and speciation, and the toolbox of proteins and enzymes and widgets in a tiny cell. There are times when the narration alludes to the winners of the Nobel Prize, the highest prize given to any scientist. The tale itself is based on some guesses (hypotheses) in chordate evolution, our evolution, that we vertebrates are the descendants of a sea squirt that did not grow up but kept right on swimming. While this guess was popular in the past, it has been questioned in the present, because that is the nature of the scientific process.

The idea I had was to encourage scientific literacy, wonder, and curiosity, not through a textbook but rather within the context of a story told to a child. I have seen children follow the organized march of ants in the backyard and test how they can create ant chaos. I have heard them ask, Who painted the rainbow on the sky? Why did the motor of the cat start up when he was scratched behind his ears? And that rock? Why did it fall from the ledge, but the feather flies, fluttering in the wind until caught in the clutches of a spider's web? How could that bright orange sea star stick to that rock when the waves come rolling? And what makes that jellyfish glow in the dark? How come all the color we see in daylight fades to gray in darkness? How did the world happen? How come Grandma died? What makes me a person?

For all that, for curosity, for wonder, for the thrill of discovery, for the power of doubt and of being so often wrong and sometimes right yet still eager to find, follow, and strive for understanding of the world around and in us—for that I wrote this little story. For all the unabashed biology geeks and nerds (you know who you are), this story is for you.

Contents

1

Siona's Misadventures at the Beach

SIONA THE HUMAN GIRL FOLLOWED the path of footprints in the sand. Two gulls, the remnants of dinosaurs, sailed through the air, their transit beneath the sun casting shadows on the path. A third gull screeched in pursuit. Siona jumped but held her ground on the loose sand. Beyond the beach a drowned gull rolled in the cradle of the sea. Its webbed feet waved above the water. They were orange, like carrots. Siona's brow creased. Behind her the dune towered, nearly a cliff. She licked her lips and swallowed. The salt in the air made her thirsty. She pulled her backpack from her shoulders and lifted the large water bottle that her mother had insisted she take and took a gulp of the lukewarm water. Turning to face the dune, Siona considered the odds of escape from the beach. She could climb the driftwood there and grab the clumps of seagrass growing in patches on the cliff. The seagrass would likely cut into the palms of her hands, but if she moved fast, she wouldn't feel it until she came to a stop. By then she would be up and over and running across the dunes.

She stepped back to reevaluate her path up the driftwood. Old gray trunks, the relics of a forest, rested against the sandy cliff—monstrous gray roots severed from the trunks and tipped upside down or on their sides, the furniture of giants following a tumultuous tea party. Siona imagined the giants with their seaweed tea and clam crackers and sand-baked toasts, until, roused by the winds, they changed from rowdy to fierce.

Siona heard her mother call her name in the usual way, stretching the syllables, starting with "Sea" followed by the long breath of "Oh" and ending with an abrupt "Nuh."

"Siona, over here," her mother called, standing on the rock above the tide pools like an ambulatory mermaid, as if all the time she spent by the ocean had made her a creature of the sea. "The sea, my life's passion," Siona had heard her mother say, "the love of my life." Most likely a sea cucumber had captured her mother's attention. Siona sighed and glanced back to the escape route. Her mother called again.

Siona took a deep breath and knelt in the sand, readjusting the contents in her backpack, pushing her book under her sweatshirt to make room for the water bottle. She could have stayed at home with her books for company or made her dad's favorite cookies with her best friend Gracie Alice. But now she knelt in the sand and zipped up her backpack. She swung it to her shoulders and winced at the weight of the water. She traversed the beach to her mother, counting each step from the dune. When she crossed from the dry sand to the wet, her heart pounded, matching the sound of the breakers offshore. She joined her mother at the brink of a rocky tide pool. Fifty-nine steps from the driftwood furniture. Her mother smiled and reached over to tousle Siona's hair. Siona stared down at her toes.

Below them, the salt sea pool was a mirror. Across the surface, clouds ambled in a line. Gulls sailed above the clouds. Beneath the surface of the water, the tentacles of anemones radiated the green rays of sunken suns among armored chitons. Orange and purple sea stars clung to the rocks between black mussels and white barnacles. Her mother motioned to the shallow pool below, her reflection pointing to Siona's.

"Look, my little larva, there we are too!"

Siona's reflection frowned, unsteady in the sudden breeze. She bent to pick up a pebble, holding it above the pool. Her image below mocked her movements. Her arms wavered. She dropped the pebble. The clouds scattered and the birds disappeared. Her reflection fled from the scene and vanished into the sand and stones. She raised a hand to shield her eyes from the noontime sun. Driven by friction between air and water, the waves rolled, pounding the shore with stochastic repetition. In the middle of the beach a flock of gulls squabbled over a quarter of a crab.

Siona shuddered. She closed her eyes and covered her ears with her hands.

"Are you all right?" asked her mother.

Siona nodded. She uncovered her ears, wincing at the thunder of the breakers.

Her mother knelt down in the sand before her daughter. "Are you sure?"

Siona nodded again.

"Would you like to go swimming?" asked her mother.

"I can't," said Siona, shaking her head. She glanced down the beach to the gulls, busy making smaller fractions of the crab.

"We can jump the waves together like we used to do," said Siona's mother. "How long has it been now?" She stared down at her watch, as if it could tell the time of past events. "Has it been since the retreat last year? Don't you want to swim in the ocean again?"

"I can't," Siona repeated, rubbing her nose. The breeze carried the faint scent of rotten eggs.

It smelled like the sea. It smelled of earth, of wind, of life, and of what follows that.

Siona dug her toes into the sand and squinted down the beach. At the far end, a man and woman sat anchored on the black rocks above the tide, holding hands. At the base of the rocks, an elderly couple filled two folding chairs beneath a blue umbrella. Four young children splashed in and out of the waves, their hoots and shouts a challenge to the cries of the gulls.

"See, that's what happens to grown-ups. They don't swim anymore. They're stuck on the rocks or on the beach," said Siona, pointing with a sandy finger. "Only little kids swim." She dug her toes deeper into the sand. "And I'm eleven now," she added.

"That's right, my little larva. You're growing up."

"Well, I'm about 58 percent grown-up right now," said Siona. "And I'm not 100 percent sure when I'll be fully grown-up."

Her mother crossed her arms in front of her chest. "I don't think you should worry about that. One day you're a little larva, and the next thing you know, you're 100 percent grown-up." She looked down at her watch again. "Well, I won't have time to go swimming now anyway."

Siona glanced at the waves, growing restless. A deep bass thundered. Rocks and pebbles clattered and rattled in the sea. Offshore, a wave towered—a giant. Siona swallowed, turned, and sprinted to the piled driftwood at the base of the cliff. She jumped on top of an old gray log. In her flight, she had counted forty-two steps. Quelled by the outgoing flow of the previous breaker, the giant dwarfed.

Her mother trotted across the beach after Siona, a perplexed expression on her face. Siona's cheeks were pale as she turned to face the sea, balancing on the log. Where the wave had journeyed up the shore, a shell rested in a ribbon of foam. Siona pointed to the shell, and her mother, after a quick glance out across the waves, strode to the froth the sea had left behind. Siona followed. Her mother rolled up the sleeves of her sweatshirt, on the back of which large blue letters proclaimed "Property of Echo Bay Marine Biology Lab."

Siona peeked around her mother and knelt to lift the shell from the sand. She held it in the palms of her hands. It was white, luminous, broken—the top of the shell cracked in half. The remainder flapped on a ruined hinge. Inside the shell, nestled above the iridescent mother of pearl, the gray mass of the creature clung. Siona looked up at her mother. "Can we help it?" she asked.

Her mother knelt in the sand and placed an arm over Siona's shoulders. She shook her head.

"That's the problem with the sea," said Siona, wiping one hand on her shorts. "It's a monster."

"What? A monster?" said her mother, glancing to the sea. Nothing out of the ordinary rose from the waves.

Siona watched the waves repeat, her face grim. She carried the shell to the still water of the tide pool and lowered it to the surface of the water. A broken raft, the shell tipped, took on water, and sank. Siona knelt at the edge of the pool. Her mother joined her. Their reflections hovered over the broken shell. In reply, the creature winked gray in the colored nacre of its shell.

"Maybe it broke its shell to protect someone else," said Siona, standing up.

"Maybe," said her mother, rising to stand by her daughter. "Maybe we are looking at one heroic mollusk, one that sacrificed herself so that others could live. And I bet she had a great life and lots of children too."

"Happy as a clam," said Siona. The bulbous mass of the creature rolled from the shell. Adrift in the tide pool, it bobbed across the sandy bottom until it was intercepted by a crab. Siona cried. "There is no one to protect her." She covered her eyes with her hands. Down the beach, the gulls lifted into the air, the crab fractions divided into their ranks.

Her mother pulled Siona from the pool. "It's the circle of life," her mother was saying. "What is made is taken; what is taken gives, and more is made." She knelt in the sand before her daughter. "Do you understand?" Siona nodded. "Good, good. I'm glad you understand." Her mother stood up and brushed the sand from her knees. "Come with me; keep me company."

Siona's mother started walking and talking about the samples she needed to collect from the microbial mats that blanketed the rocks of the tide pools. "Over there," she said, pointing. They were of great antiquity and layered like lasagna. Each living layer was its own habitat of microbes, with the aerobic on the outside and the anaerobic on the inside. And between the layers at the redox boundary was evidence for the fusion of symbiotic partners and the generation of the very first eukaryotic creature. She had only a few more tests to do to confirm her hypothesis. It would be a breakthrough in metabolic evolution. And today, for an hour or two, the tide would be low and the mats exposed. The tide would not be this low again for another year. Siona's mother took a deep breath, her eyes bright and her cheeks flushed.

"And we have to go closer to the sea?" Siona's hands trembled.

"Yes," said her mother, walking faster.

"I'd like to, but ..." Siona swallowed, watching the waves pound the rocks offshore. "I brought my book. That log over there looks like a good place to read." She pointed away from the sea to the pile of driftwood nestled below the dune.

Her mother came to a stop and held out her hand. "Please come with me. I'd like to show you something."

Siona swallowed again. "But the book I'm reading is about a werewolf guy who accidentally falls in love with a vampire girl."

"Oh no!" said her mother. "That does not bode well!"

"And the werewolf also happens to be magical. And the vampire girl is a princess. And by chance they have a little vampwolf daughter that they named Matilde."

"That is some story!" said her mother, holding out her hand in the empty space between them.

Siona took a deep breath. "Okay, show me," she said.

Siona followed her mother to the rocks on the opposite side of the beach, away from where the children and the two couples had made their encampments. Siona's mother jumped out on the rocks and walked with sure steps. Siona glanced back to the driftwood beneath the sandy cliff and then clambered over the rocks after her mother. They walked over the markings of time. Siona peered down to a pedestal of rock inscribed with the stony autobiographies of three small trilobites. Two steps later, another story was written in the rock about a family of *Wiwaxia* gathered with a lone *Hallucigenia*, as if to compare their armored appendages. The fossils littered the rocks, the petroglyphs of the ancients.

Siona's mother pointed to each—the feathers and fronds of *Charnia masoni*, the ovals of *Dickinsonia costata*, and the stars of unknown fossils. On the lower layers of the rock, waves, whirls, and filamentous etchings marked earlier undertakings in the grand experiment of life. Far below from where the girl and woman paused, deep in the sedimentary slop, were the earliest of all—the molecules of life brought together and propagated by events so improbable that one might venture to use the word *miraculous*. The air was heavy with the scent of microbial mats.

The woman continued on her way with Siona following. They walked between pools of water and muck until they reached the mats. Siona's mother sat down on a rock and opened her backpack. She pulled on her sea-green nitrile gloves and set up the cryogenic rack with microcentrifuge tubes. She labeled each tube with a black marker. Next, she pulled out the gauged pipette that she had designed back in graduate school. She called it her "slime collector." She looked at her watch and, with a deep breath, collected the first sample of slime.

Siona held her nose and edged away from the sea, almost tripping into a tide pool. She leaned forward, hovering over the pool. Her image frowned back. On the still water, a plane overhead zoomed past. She knelt down and stirred the water with the tip of her finger. Her image rippled. A startled school of small fish sped away, careening as one around a curve in the pool. One little fish swam off by itself. It swam in a tight little circle and jumped from the water, splashing back down with a little plop, only to leap up again. Plop. It swam a crooked figure eight and then hastened off away from the other fish on its lonesome journey.

Below where the fish had swum its circle, Siona saw something shine silver. She called to her mother, who looked down at her watch and pipetted another sample. Drops of sweat rested on her mother's brow. Siona called again, louder this time. Her mother rose from the microbial mats, removing her gloves. She walked to the edge of the pool to stand beside Siona, who pointed to the shiny thing under the water at the base of a rock.

"Why don't you reach in and grab it?" asked her mother. "It will be okay. It won't bite you."

Siona shook her head. "Could you get it, please?"

Her mother bent down and reached into the cool water of the pool.

She pulled out a silver coin. She held it in the palm of her hand and turned it over. Heads. Tails. It was a quarter. She handed it to Siona and scrambled back over to the mats.

"Thank you. I can give this quarter back to you the next time you park downtown and forget the coins again."

"I would appreciate that," said her mother, collecting another sample. "Thank you," she added.

Siona tossed the coin, catching it in the palm of her hand. "Heads," she said. Toss. "Heads again." Toss again. "Heads." Again. Heads. Heads, heads, heads, heads.

"There is something wrong with this coin," Siona said. "I got heads at least a million times."

"A million times?" asked her mother, labeling another tube.

"Well, more like twenty times." Siona studied the coin, turning it over. On one side the profile of George Washington. In God We Trust. Heads. On the other, the Great Sand Dunes, 2014. Tails.

Siona's mother took off her gloves and reached into her backpack, pulling out a calculator. She pressed the keypad and then looked up. "The chance of a fair coin ending up heads twenty times in a row is one out of one million forty-eight thousand five hundred seventy-six to be exact."

"Isn't that impossible?"

"Not impossible; the chances are one in one million forty-eight thousand five hundred seventy six," repeated her mother, looking at her watch and collecting another sample. "There's a 50 percent chance that the next one will be tails."

Siona tossed the coin again. She missed it on its descent, and it fell back into the pool, partially slipping under a rock. Siona pointed to the coin. "You were right!" she cried. "This time it came up tails."

Siona reached into the water to collect the coin, pushing the rock aside. There was a flurry of movement where the rock had been. A ragworm wiggled and twisted. It opened its fangs wide and snapped them shut. Siona flapped her right hand. A golden-brown ragworm clung to the tip of her middle finger. She screamed and, slipping on a clump of algae, fell into the shallow pool. The palm of her left hand landed squarely on what looked like a white plastic bag. With the force of her fall, a jet of seawater squirted from the bag, striking her in the mouth, turning her scream into a sputter. Now returned to water, the worm made a rapid departure from her finger, leaving a bright red spot. She screamed again. Her mother grabbed Siona's arm and pulled her from the pool.

Siona cried, trying to dry her mouth with a wet sleeve. "You're never around when I need you!"

"I'm right here now."

"The ocean hates me!" Siona pointed her middle finger at her mother, showing the bloody tip. "I want to go home! I know you have important things to do, but can we please go home?"

The elderly couple under the umbrella and the children playing in the water stared in Siona's direction. The younger couple, moments earlier absorbed in a kiss, separated from their embrace. The man cast a glance of annoyance at Siona.

"It's okay; it's okay," said Siona's mother. "Here, let me take a look at your finger."

Siona pointed her middle finger again. Her mother ignored the gesture and held Siona's hand in hers, inspecting the wound. "It looks like a tiny nip from a ragworm. It's nothing to worry about. I'll get a bandage and some disinfectant, and it will be all good."

"It hurts," whimpered Siona. She wiped her eyes with her wet sleeve. "That ragworm and the entire ocean must hate me."

Siona's mother reached into her backpack and pulled out the disinfectant. "The ragworm does not hate you. Neither does the ocean. The worm was just defending itself. It was probably more afraid of you than you were of it." She sprayed the disinfectant on the wound and pulled out a yellow bandage decorated with shells. She let the disinfectant dry and then wrapped Siona's finger with the bandage. She placed her hands on Siona's shoulders. "All better now?"

Siona pointed with her bandaged finger to the thing that looked like a white plastic bag with two openings like straws on top. "Is it okay? That white plastic-bag-like thing that tried to drown me. I might have smashed it. Is it okay?" She sniffled.

Her mother knelt down and looked at the white creature in the water. "Oh," she said, "it's a sea squirt. It looks a bit squished, but its tunic is okay. Those squirt tunics are a wonder. They're made out of cellulose." The woman wiped her hair from her forehead. She reached into the water and propped up the bag-like creature, glancing at her watch. "Darn, I missed a time point." She scrambled back to the microbial mats and pulled on her gloves. She dove her pipette down, pulling out a hunk of slime. She flipped open the cap of a microcentrifuge tube with a deft movement of her thumb, ejected the slime-filled pipette tip in the tube, and snapped the cap in place. She looked back to Siona. "Does your finger feel better?" she called.

"No." Siona shook her head. "It hurts. Can we go home soon, please?"

Siona's mother blinked. Her shoulders dropped. Her forehead creased. The second hand on her watch ticked off the time. She bit her lip. "Honey …" she said collecting another sample of slime. "I'll be right there. I'm sorry …" Another sample was collected. "These creatures in the sea are like us, and we are like them. We're like family." Another slime core collected.

"We are family," repeated Siona in a whisper as her mother checked the time. She sat on the hard black rock, holding her hand. Salty tears welled up in her eyes, dropping to her wet sleeves. She called out louder so her mother could hear this time. "And I lost the quarter. The one thing we found that was helpful. You never have any coins when you park the car downtown!"

"Oh, my little larva," said Siona's mother, looking at her watch and driving the gauged pipette down into the microbial mat, "don't worry about the quarter. I'm so sorry that I wasn't right there when you needed me." She deposited another sample into a microcentrifuge tube. "Can you forgive me? Please?"

"I don't want to be by the ocean. I want to read my book." Siona stared at the rocks below. "My book has never bitten me, and it's about vampires and werewolves!"

Siona's mother paused, looking up at the sky. She pulled off her gloves and put them beside her pipette. Sighing, she rose and crossed the black rock to sit beside her daughter. "Look at me," she said. "I know that this is hard for you." She took a deep breath. "I need you to be brave. I need another hour. What I'm doing is … is important for my career and everything that I've worked for so hard. I need one more hour. Can you please be brave for me?"

"Yes, I'll be brave," said Siona to the rocks below.

"Thank you, my little larva," said her mother. "You are brave. I'll make you a hot chocolate and tell you a story when we get home." Siona's mother went back to the mats. She put her gloves back on, pulling them on so hard that the nitrile snapped back, slapping her wrists. "I can pipette," she whispered to the microbial mats below, "but I suck as a mother."

Siona did not talk during the car ride home. Her mother talked the entire time, giving instructions to her headset on how the samples should be stored and processed. "Yes. Yes in the minus eighty freezer for the 'D' samples. All samples in the tubes labeled 'B' should be fixed in paraformaldehyde and sent over to the electron microscopy lab. The samples labeled 'A' need to go to Ricky in the Mass Spec Core for analysis. But most important of all, ASAP, hand-deliver the samples labeled 'C' to Dr. Irawit. Yes, Yes. She is in the lab right now. Yes, the plates are coated and ready … No, I can't be there … But Dr. Irawit, she'll know what to do … That's right … electrochemiluminescent quantitation of the histidine kinase subtypes. Biomarkers of evolution … This could be a huge. A breakthrough … And could you do me another favor?" she whispered to the recipient on the other side of her headset. "My daughter … run-in with a ragworm … I need to take her home. Can you stop by … pick up the samples? I won't forget this. Thank you."

Thirty minutes later, Siona's mother parked the car in the driveway, and the two headed up the walkway to the front door. Two graduate students jumped up from the front steps. "Dr. Seaton!" they called, bounding down the steps.

Siona's mother gave them each a hug. "I owe you," she said.

"So, a ragworm got you? Is that right?" asked one of the students. Siona pointed her middle finger. The students laughed. "Been there!"

Siona's mother handed the students the cryogenic rack of microcentrifuge tubes. "Handle with care," she said. "This could change everything."

The students gave their assurances, and Siona's mother watched them depart. She unlocked the front door and held it open.

Siona crossed the threshold, her head hanging. "I'm sorry," she said. "I'm sorry I was bitten by a ragworm."

Siona's mother shook her head. "You don't have to be sorry." She went to the kitchen and returned a few minutes later with a mug of hot chocolate. She maneuvered her daughter to a large rocking chair, made by Siona's grandfather, and placed the hot chocolate on a coaster on the end table. They sat together, rocking. Siona raised her hand to inspect her finger, and she leaned her head onto her mother's shoulder.

"Are you ready to hear a story?" asked her mother.

"*Oh!* You'll tell me a story?" asked Siona. "Like you used to when you weren't so busy all the time?"

Her mother winced but nodded. "Long ago," she began, "strange and wondrous creatures lived. In fact, there was one little creature named Siona, just like you."

"Like me?" asked Siona.

"Yes," said her mother, "this will be the story of Siona and her adventures."

"Will there be magic in the story?"

"Yes," said Siona's mother, "the miraculous magic of math and science."

"Will it be hard for me to understand?" asked Siona.

"Not at all," replied her mother.

"Is this going to be a scary story?" asked Siona, gripping the curved armrest.

"Only sometimes," replied her mother. "This will be a story about us, about you."

"About us?" asked Siona. "And me?"

Her mother nodded. "Had it not been for Siona, our story would have been very different. In fact, I would not be telling you this tale, and you would not be here to hear it."

2

Long Ago

ONCE UPON A TIME, 521.2 million years ago, long before you were born, in one corner of an immense universe—one perhaps of many of such things that might be there but that we could only calculate—in the suburbs of a galaxy called the Milky Way, a nearly middle-aged rocky planet, the distant progeny of a small dot of mass from the beginning of time, spun on its axis, rotating around a small but bright star, just at the right distance, where it was not too hot or too cold or too irradiated. On this rock of a planet, a precious substance made of two simple atoms covered much of the surface, blue to the eye, wet to the touch, the greatest of all lifegiving incubators—water. The water sloshed, crashing in rolling waves against rocky shores, molding land and life. At the fringes of this mighty sea, small tide pools nestled in the rocks like watery islands. And there, in one tide pool, was the one thing needed for our story to begin—an egg.

You likely have seen many eggs before, such as chicken eggs on the kitchen counter, or frog eggs at the edge of a pond, or maybe even fish eggs stuck to the aquarium wall. But this egg was shaped like a star, with tiny points all around. But what was inside this egg? A chicken? A frog? Maybe a fish? No, not those creatures. Those creatures had not yet flown, hopped, or swum on this planet yet.

Inside that egg was a tiny creature, a sea squirt larva. Her name was Siona, Siona the Sea Squirt. And this is the tale of her adventures. Her adventures began even before she hatched. Before Siona was Siona, the star of her egg rolled, glowing blue, then silver, then orange, like an enchanted microscopic lantern bobbing in the water. A star-shaped sack of stuff and goo. A tiny floating universe.

But how to change from an egg to a creature; from a solitary cell to a whole bunch of cells with the audacity to join ranks and form a community, all in support of a single soul? What does an egg need? All it needs is input from the father.

Siona's egg bobbed along in the water and bumped into a creature with a long Latin name, *Primogenitus notochordus-neotenous*, though his friends all called him Propikaia. He was blessed with near-perfect symmetry, as if his left half was a mirror image of his right. To define where one might place that mirror, a slight ridge ran down the length of his glistening back to the tip of his tail. Propikaia paid no attention to the star that twinkled at his side. He was busy, working hard to release the stuff of life to usher in the next generation. In the scent of the sea, he knew a loved one was nearby with whom he could share his quest for immortality. He thrashed his tail as he aspired to fatherhood, unwittingly catching the attention of a hungry shrimp.

The shrimp lunged; its claws opened wide. Terrified, Propikaia beat the water with his tail, escaping into a forest of algae. In the fury of the shrimp's attack, there was a flurry of the fecund waters surrounding Propikaia. Siona's egg tumbled in the water. It was an accident, an improbable freak event of nature—an event so improbable that it could happen less than once in more than a billion—a horizontal gene transfer event. A bit of the stuff of life that made Propikaia transferred through the water and comingled with the stuff of life in Siona's tiny egg. And that was what Siona's egg needed—the contributions from a father.

Siona's egg sparkled. The stuff and goo in the starry egg grew expectant, like the musicians of an orchestra warming up. Their discordant notes resounded in the great hall of the egg. With the input from the father, the program began. The stuff and goo inside Siona's egg transformed, dividing into two cells; the two cells divided into four, the four to eight, the eight to sixteen, then to thirty-two, sixty-four, and on and on until what would become Siona was a big hollow blob of cells. The program grew more complex with the rhythm and pattern of an experimental score. And the cells transformed into Siona the Sea Squirt larva. She looked very much like a tadpole made of over one thousand cells. There were muscle cells to help Siona wiggle and move, brain cells or neurons to help her think and see, cells to help pump nutrients and food, cells like little soldiers to protect her from infection and foreign invaders, and even cells to help all the other cells stick together and cover her tiny body.

With all those cells, Siona was crammed in her egg. She wiggled her tail, trying to escape. She struggled against the tough and fibrous walls of her egg, pounding the walls of the egg, first with her head and then with her tail. The walls of the egg held firm. Siona snorted in the egg. She tried pounding and wiggling at the same time. That did not work either against the tough egg. She banged her head against the egg until tears filled her eyes. "Oh, I cannot stand a moment more locked up in this darn *egg!*" she cried. "*Let me out! Let me out! I need to be free!*"

Siona lunged forward in desperation. The fibrous vitelline wall of her protective egg ruptured. And Siona the Sea Squirt squirted right out of the egg, headfirst, tumbling into a tide pool at the edge of the pounding sea. Released from her tiny egg, Siona's universe expanded by more than seven orders of magnitude, or 10 times 10 times 10 times 10 times 10 times 10 times 10 times. That was a good thing because in a nearby tiny tide pool, sea squirt larvae floated listlessly among the dead and dying—the tiny tide pool unable to sustain the growing population of squirts. Not only did a planet have to be at the right distance from its star, but a tide pool had to be the right size too.

Siona surveyed her new home. She was not much more than a dot with a tail in all those gallons of water. Water gurgled all around, a consequence of chemistry and the gravitational tug of the planet, a gift of water bearing carbonaceous asteroids since the planet's inception. Siona closed her eyes, basking in the water. She swam a tight, tiny perfect circle, two loop the loops, followed by four figure eights. Next, she swam as fast as she could away from the remains of her broken egg, only to let herself tumble down through the water, barrel-rolling in her descent. Three cone-shaped *Hyoliths* regarded Siona from the tide pool floor. They dragged their shell-covered bodies across the sand on thin arms, moving a millimeter a minute. They sighed when Siona did another perfect circle. A wormish creature raised its proboscis from its shelly home, buried in the sand, to watch Siona swim. Three sea squirt larvae, who had hatched two days earlier, scrutinized Siona as she sailed past.

Siona was in her element. She wiggled, shaking off the remaining clumps of fibrous vitelline. With a flick of her tail, she glided through the water, the mighty rhythm of life surging in her tiny body, as forceful and as driven as the tide. The water parted to let the little larva pass.

Siona rolled on her back, swimming upside down. The vacant eggs of sea squirt larvae bobbed on the surface of the water, turning into tiny prisms. They gave birth to fleeting rainbows. Had Siona had a jaw, it would have dropped. But jaws had not yet evolved. Instead, her little ocelli eyes flashed in the sun. Siona had the right stuff to see. That's how she could see the rainbows. Imagine the silence of a tree crashing to the forest floor if you had no ears.

"Oh!" she cried, as the rays of violet, blue, green, yellow, and red danced across the surface of the water. "Look at all the colors!" she exclaimed to three squirt larvae who were staring with abandoned longing at a big black rock below.

"What?" replied one of the three, not taking his gaze from the rock. "What colors?"

Siona shrugged and rolled in the water, diving to the bottom of the tide pool. She swam through clumps of red and green algae and alongside a bright purple-and-yellow creature as it crept across the black rocks. A snail with a bright blue shell caught her attention. The snail looked back at Siona with one eye on the tip of his antenna. He gave her a green-lipped smile. Siona swam in tight spirals, following the curves of the snail's shell. The shell's color was a function of the wavelength of light, of tiny waves reflected at 465 nanometers from peak to peak—each nanometer only one-billionth of a meter and much smaller than one-sixteenth of an inch. And that was the color blue. From the red algae, light ricocheted in waves at 630 nanometers, and from the green clumps of algae, the light bounced off at 525 nanometers.

And all that from the single star of the solar system, some ninety-three million miles away, where the photons of light escaped as packets of energy, waves, and particles to bombard and bounce from the shell of a snail, only to be captured and absorbed by specialized photoreceptor cells in Siona's ocelli eyes, each carefully tuned to the wavelengths of the light—that was how she saw the world in color.

She blinked, dashing across the bottom of the pool over brown, gray, and purple rocks. She sailed over the speckled sand, its silica the contribution of ancient diatoms, radiolarians, and sponges, creatures gifted in the sequestration of silicon acid. To her left, a cluster of still-living diatoms sparkled like glitter, each encased in a microscopic greenhouse of silica glass.

Siona raced over a cluster of red rocks covered with stripes of oozing green slime. Red, green, red, green—a pulsing strobe of color before her eyes as she fled past. Back she bolted over a series of large black rocks. Their beauty caught her by surprise, as if their density and darkness held some unknown truth of her destiny. She slowed, hovering over the allure of the dark rocks below. She glanced back at the three squirt larvae. They still floated over the black rock to her right, mesmerized. She felt that there was something important, something that she should know. But she could not quite put her tail on it.

A rotifer twirled past, two wheels spinning on its head, interrupting her thoughts. She felt dizzy watching them whirl. The creature compressed its body into a ball, rolling in the water. Bam! It exploded, elongating to a baseball bat.

"Oh my! Oh my!" Siona giggled.

The single rotifer was joined by a half dozen others of its kind. They squeezed into little balls. And bam! They became long like baseball bats. Ball. Bat. Ball. Bat. Ball. Bat. Siona found that she could tickle the rotifers with her tail and make them change from tiny balls to long bats or from long bats to tiny balls.

"Wow! How can you do that? How can you get round and long like that so fast?"

"Because we have the wee, teeny, tiny widgets that help us move!" cried the first rotifer in a shrill voice.

"Widget? What do you mean? What's a widget?" asked Siona.

The second rotifer compressed to a ball and expanded to a bat as he cried, "Almost everything that we can do is because of our widgets within!"

"Where would we be without our widgets?" squeaked the third and fourth rotifers together.

"No, no, it's not where would we be, but *what* could we be without our widgets!" cried the fifth rotifer, exploding from a compressed tiny ball into a long bat.

"You have the widgets too!" cried the sixth rotifer to Siona.

"And your widgets must be super-special, because I've never seen a sea squirt larva swim even a single loop the loop!" cried the seventh rotifer, twirling past.

"Really? I have widgets too?" Siona looked back at her tail, searching for her widgets.

The widgets were proteins. They were of the elements—of earth, water, and air. Of amino acids. Of carbon, hydrogen, oxygen, nitrogen, and sulfur, stuck together by the fire in her cells like beads stitched in a string. Some of her widgets were coils, some were sheets, some were long rods, and others were globular. Like little biological machines, the widgets, or proteins, did all sorts of stuff in and around Siona's cells. Some of the widgets were like little scissors, cutting other proteins. Others were like sewing machines, stitching other widgets together. Some widgets were enzymes that catalyzed reactions, lowering the activation energy to make a specific reaction more likely. In Siona's long tail, little protein motors raced along highways made of yet other protein widgets, carrying cargo down her tail just like trucks and cars. There were pumps, channels, and transporters, all made of protein widgets designed to bring good things in and take bad things out of Siona's cells. There were receptor widgets that received special messages from other cells and even from the world around. So if Siona were to swim into a rock with a thump, the thump would trigger a whole cascade of changes in her widgets, like one domino knocking into another. And Siona would know that she had struck a rock. Ouch!

Siona wiggled her tail in the water; the widgets actin and myosin slid by each other as her muscles contracted. The rotifers smiled, and with their own actin and myosin widgets, they contracted to wee balls. Over the next 521 million years, these widgets would stay pretty much the same and would be used someday by a pitcher throwing a fast ball or sprinter racing for a new world record.

Siona touched two round rotifers that were compressed into tiny balls with the tip of her tail. "Show me what your widgets can do!" she cried. Inside the rotifers, the tubulin widgets came into play. With electrifying speed the tubulins joined, one on top of the other, polymerizing into long filamentous microtubule widgets, like tiny subcellular bones that grew longer in an instant. The rotifers expanded into long bats. When Siona's tail sailed past the rotifers again, the microtubules depolymerized, collapsed, and shed the tubulin subunits. The rotifers contracted, floating ball-like in the water again.

"Show us what your widgets can do!" cried one of the rotifers.

"Show us! Show us what your widgets can do!" cried all the rotifers, egging her on. Siona looked up. She whipped her tail, her widgets in full force. She swam straight up. Up, out of the water, she streaked. Siona gasped in the unkind air, losing control of her widgets. Back down she fell, belly-flopping on the surface of the water and tumbling to the rotifers below.

The rotifers screamed with laughter. "You are too funny!" they cried.

"Wow! I wish I had been able to see that!" said Siona, dancing in the water between the rotifers. She swished her tail. "I want to see how fast I can swim!" She plunged through the water, swimming with the might of her widgets. Her speed was her glory; the wake behind, her triumph; the water rushing past, her Eden.

She plowed headlong into the waves, the waves of a song. The melody brought her to a standstill. Siona hesitated, listening. She flicked her tail and turned in a tight circle, searching for ... what? There. There it was again. A song. In the water, the notes surrounded her. She could almost feel them, bumping into her tail. She hovered in the water, floating in the song flooding the water. Siona's peristaltic heart squeezed faster. She gulped. She recognized the tone, the cadence. It was her mother.

She heard her mother sing from far away, the medium of water a great conductor of sound. Siona cringed at the words. "Find a lovely rock, my little larvae. It's time for all the swimming to stop! It's time to anchor to a rock." The song rolled in waves. And in reply, Siona heard the other sea squirt larvae sing:

> Find a rock,
> Find a rock
> On which to dock
> On which to grow.
> This is all we need to know.

Siona did not know the words to the song.

3

Positively Phototactic

THE SEA SQUIRT LARVAE HOVERED together, a floating congregation. Siona edged her way over to the flock and hovered at the outskirts. Many of them looked at her askance. She heard one whisper, "I thought that egg was a dud." Another replied, "She looks … weird."

Siona did not feel weird when she swam. So she barrel-rolled in the water and swam a little circle and then a bigger circle around all the other larvae gathered together. She swam upside down, rolling from side to side in the water. She tickled a rotifer that twirled past. She heard more murmurs from the others. "She looks different," and "Her head is too big," and "Her tail is odd." Siona looked at her tail. She did not see anything wrong with her tail. She liked her tail. She smiled, giving her tail a little flick. The water rippled, carrying more comments.

"What is wrong with that larva?"

"Why is she swimming in circles and upside down?"

"She should stop swimming and look for a rock, like us." There was a pause. "She is not like us."

Siona hesitated. The smile vanished from her face.

"Weirdo," said another larva. The word cut through the water. Siona's tail drooped.

"Hey, you!" called a large larva with a skinny tail. "Stop swimming around, and get over here."

Siona looked down at the larva and pointed to herself with her tail.

"Yes, that's right. I mean you. You. The one with the big tail. Come over here."

Siona swam to the skinny-tailed squirt.

"Okay," said Skinny, "let's practice being negatively phototactic." There were murmurs of approval. The other larvae nodded. Siona blinked.

"Me first! Me first!" cried another big larva. "I know exactly what to do." He had bright blue whiskers on the tip his head. He swam down, aiming for a large black rock. Siona noted that his trajectory was a near perfect forty-five-degree angle from the surface of the water, as if he were integrating the number of photons over time during his descent. He touched his head to the rock below. A cheer rose from the others. "Well done, Blue! That was superb!" Blue smiled as he returned to the others.

The next larva to try was a tiny little thing. She whipped her tail madly right and left. Siona watched Tiny's tail. The movements hardly propelled the poor squirt forward. At last, little Tiny gave up. Floating on her side, she cried, and blue whiskers dripped from her head. The other larvae were quiet. They looked down at their sibling, halfway to the rocks.

"Okay, okay," said Skinny. "Now you know what not to do. That's how you can end up." There was a cry from Tiny. "Now, let's move over to some other rocks. Nothing can be done for Tiny." He swam away, and the other larvae followed him—all but Siona; she dove down to Tiny.

"I think I know what's wrong," said Siona.

"What's wrong," cried Tiny, "is that I can't make it to the rocks. And if I can't make it to the rocks then … then … I don't make it at all!" Tiny cried blue tears.

"It's your tail," said Siona. "You're overworking your tail. Don't move it so far from side to side. See? Look," she said, demonstrating how a tiny wiggle could propel her forward but a big wide waggle of her tail just fanned the water, creating drag. "You give it a try."

Tiny sighed. "I'm not sure I can."

"I'll give you a push."

Tiny wiggled.

Siona pushed. "Good job, good job," Siona said. "Try not to wiggle so wide." When she felt Tiny move forward on her own, Siona stopped pushing and swam close behind. "You are almost there to the others!"

"Keep pushing me," cried Tiny, her tail swishing with efficiency through the water. "I can feel you pushing."

"I'm not pushing anymore. You're on your own."

"I can't be."

"You can!"

"Can't."

Siona swam to Tiny's side. "Can."

Tiny grinned wide. And the two larvae swam side by side by the power of their mighty tails. Siona smiled as she watched Tiny join the others, their eyes blinking. They flicked their tails and touched Tiny in welcome with their heads. Tiny smiled and, with her head held high, she swam an efficient circle around the others as they cheered.

Skinny, his tail a gavel, struck the water with a thump. "All right, all right! Settle down." He looked over at Siona. "Okay, you with the big tail … and head, it's your turn."

"You can call me Siona."

"Show them what you can do," whispered Tiny to Siona. "Show them how you can swim!"

Siona nodded. *I'll show them what my widgets can do!* Siona swam down at a perfect forty-five-degree angle, approaching a large black rock. She heard cheers from above. Before she reached the rock, she turned, shooting straight up, passing the others on her ascent, heading to where the sunlight danced in bright coils on the surface of the water.

"You're going the wrong way!" yelled Skinny.

"She's positively phototactic, not negatively phototactic," yelled another. "What's wrong with that squirt!"

Siona leaped from the water. The others gasped. A second passed and then another. Down Siona came, hurtling past the other larvae. They scattered, tumbling in the turbulence of Siona's tail. Three of them collided, knocking their heads together. They screamed. Siona barrel-rolled and came to a stop. There was a hush. At the bottom of the pool, the three stricken squirts lay on their sides. Siona dove straight down, her tail beating.

"I'm sorry! I'm sorry! I didn't mean to hurt you," she cried to the stunned squirts. She stopped before the first of the injured squirts and gently lifted the poor creature with her head.

"Get away from me!" bawled the squirt, recovering enough to speed away and hide behind a clump of algae.

"I'm so sorry!" said Siona, turning to the other two. One had a cut on its tail. The other had a scratch that zigzagged across its head. Siona covered her eyes with her tail.

"Siona, please move away from the squirts," said Skinny.

Siona lifted her tail from her eyes. Skinny and Blue glared at her. "I'm so sorry," she repeated.

Skinny turned to Blue. "You need to use your nanoscale whiskers and special cellulose blend to fix up those squirts before it's too late."

Blue swam to the injured squirts and touched them with his head, transferring the blue nanoscale whiskers and cellulose blend to their injuries. The wounds turned blue, and the squirts woke, wiggling from the sand.

"Can I help? Is there something that I can do," Siona asked in a whisper, following after Skinny, Blue, and the three injured squirts that labored to make their way back to others.

Tiny swam out to meet them, and she touched her head to the damaged squirts, adding more nanoscale whiskers. "It will help them heal," she told Siona.

Siona's head dropped. She sighed. She swam to join the others, but a tail blocked her way.

"Not you," said Skinny.

"It was an accident," whispered Siona. "I didn't mean to hurt anyone."

"Well, you did!" whimpered one of the injured squirts.

"I wanted to show you what my widgets could do," said Siona, peering over Skinny's tail. "Are you all right?"

"No! I'm not all right," wailed the injured squirt.

"Neither am I," sniveled the second.

"You don't belong here!" howled the third. "Go away!"

Siona hung her head.

A dozen rotifers twirled to Siona. "You can play with us," they cried. Siona took another look at the other larvae. She followed after the rotifers for a few swishes of her tail. She rolled upside down. The sunlight charted the topography of the waves in rings of gold and turquoise. The light and waves dropped shadows across Siona's body. She wanted to cry. She stopped swimming, and she sank, drifting down.

Siona heard a long wail beneath her from the bottom of the pool. Another creature was crying. Siona somersaulted in the water, ending right side up. Was someone hurt? She scanned the rocks below. There on a red rock covered with stripes of green slime, a lone little squirt wiggled, its head stuck to the rock. On one side of the squirt, a stripe of green slime oozed. The squirt whimpered, "Help me, help me." Siona approached, her eyes wide. At the base of the red rock, three translucent squirt carcasses drifted across the sand.

"It burns! It burns!" screamed the squirt.

"What burns?" asked Siona, as she reached for the squirt with her tail to give some comfort.

"The rock, the rock! I chose the wrong rock!" cried the tiny squirt. "Get me off this rock!"

Siona touched the tip of her tail to the red rock. Nothing happened. It felt like a rock. Maybe the problem was not with the rock but with the slime. Siona gave it a test with her tail.

"Ouch!" she cried. She turned to look at the tip of her tail. A dark wound burned.

"Please help me," whimpered the squirt.

"Okay," said Siona, shaking, trying not to think about the burning sensation at the tip of her tail, "I'll see if I can pry you off that rock." Hooking her tail under the squirt, she began to pry the creature from the rock. Her tail touched the slime again. Tears filled her eyes. She cried out, and with a powerful flick of her tail she freed the little larva. Off it lurched, barely able to swim. Siona swam underneath the injured creature and carried it on her back to the other larvae, her tail burning as she swam.

Siona called out. "This one is hurt too. I think he can use some nanoscale whiskers and special cellulose blend." Siona pointed with her tail to the tiny squirt's head.

Skinny and Blue darted forward, pushing the tiny squirt away from Siona.

Blue worked frantically to apply the nanoscale whiskers. "What did you do, Siona? What did you do this time?" he said.

"I … I … I was trying to help. There was this burning green slime …" Siona tried to show them the dark wound on her tail. She tried to warn them about the green slime that covered the red rocks. She pointed at the rocks with her tail. "Green and red together means danger," Siona tried to explain.

Skinny, looking at the rocks, shook his head in disbelief, squinting with his tiny ocelli eyes. What was all this fuss about color? What did that even mean? "Siona," said Skinny, "you'd better follow us." He paused, his skinny tail thumping. "Follow us from a safe distance behind. We'll take you to our mother and father. They'll explain everything."

Skinny motioned for the other larvae to follow. When they were well ahead, he called back to Siona that she should follow from behind. As the others swam on, Tiny darted back.

"Let me fix your tail," Tiny said. She touched Siona's damaged tail, applying the nanoscale whiskers and the special cellulose blend.

The pain vanished. Siona breathed with relief.

"It's medicine," said Tiny. "When you are ready to grow up, you will get your own nanoscale whiskers and special cellulose blend too."

Siona bent her tail around to take a better look. The wound on her tail was disappearing as new tissue formed. Siona wiggled her tail to test it. It worked. Her tail was on the mend. She gave Tiny a smile, and with their tails beating in unison, they swam together after the others. But the water was a great conductor of sound. Siona heard Blue, Skinny, and the others say her name and laugh. She heard the others singing the words to the song she did not know. She hung her head. "I wish I wasn't so different," she said, almost to herself.

Tiny snorted. "You aren't different, Siona," she said, beating her tiny tail. "You're special!" And off she went to join the others, singing the song that Siona did not know.

Siona followed after the others (at a safe distance), gliding over the tide pool floor. Alone. She did not care that her belly scraped along the bottom of the pool over the sand and pebbles. But as she swam, her tail got the better of her. With her tail beating, she slipped into the moment, and the unkind words of the others rolled off her back like water. She nearly closed her eyes, her tail swishing. It surprised her when she caught up with the others. They swam in a cluster beside a big black rock. Siona slowed, her peristaltic heart squeezing tight.

"All right," said Skinny to the other larvae. "Let's let Mother and Father explain how things are to Siona." The others nodded and dispersed, radiating out from the rock in all directions. Skinny, Blue, Tiny, and a score of others swam off around the bend to the left and were gone from sight.

"Siona, my little larva, please come here," sang her mother—the notes carried through the water. Siona followed the notes of her mother's song to its source. She approached the rock upon which two creatures were anchored. They looked so different from her. She could not image how they could be related. She looked like a tiny tadpole. They looked like little blue plastic bags with two straws or siphons waving from the top. Their heads were anchored to the rock below. Siona slowed her approach, her tail dragging in the water.

"Well, aren't you an odd-looking larva," stated Siona's mother's husband when Siona arrived.

"I'm odd?" asked Siona. She turned back to take a look at her tail.

"That head of yours is way too big, and so are your eyes." He squinted. "And you shall call me Sir Squirt." He waved his siphons in a circle. "Turn around so we can get a better look at you."

Siona swallowed and turned a slow circle.

"Oh, my goodness," said her mother. "I've never seen a squirt larva with such a big, long tail!"

"That must be some throwback from your family," said Sir Squirt.

"Or yours," said her mother.

"Not a chance," said Sir Squirt, thumping his plastic-bag-like tunic with one of his siphons.

"There's something wrong with my tail?" asked Siona. She held her tail as still as she could.

"There, there," said Sir Squirt to her mother, patting her with one of his siphons. "Not all larvae can be perfect. There's bound to be an oddball once in a while. Maybe she knows how to sing the rock song." He turned back to Siona, pointing at her with his left siphon. "Go ahead; sing the song."

Siona trembled. She shook her head. She did not know the words or the tune. A smile spread across her face. "But look," she said. "I can swim a loop the loop!" And she flew, an acrobat in the water, swimming one loop the loop after another.

"Oh no," cried her mother. "What are we to do?"

Sir Squirt shuddered.

"You could swim along with me. It would be fun! Let's go," said Siona, swimming circles around her mother and Sir Squirt.

"Oh, Siona, darling, we cannot move. We're sessile adults. Our heads are stuck to the rock," her mother replied, twisting as much as she could (which was not very much at all) to watch Siona as she circled.

"Do you need some help? Do you want me to pry you off that rock?"

"Oh no, we don't need any help. This is what happens when we sea squirts grow up," said her mother.

"When … sea squirts … grow … up?" stammered Siona. "Will this happen to me?"

"Yes, of course. We squirts go through metamorphosis."

Siona stopped swimming. She stared at her parents and at the rock to which their heads were securely bound. She glanced back at her tail, her jewel. It sparkled aquamarine.

"Meta … meta … what is that?"

"Metamorphosis is when our bodies change. One day you are a swimming larva, and the next thing you know, you stick your head to a rock, lose your tail, secrete your tunic, and you are a grown-up squirt with siphons. It will be wonderful!" Siona's mother said, waving her siphons.

"Stick my head to a rock and lose my tail!" cried Siona.

"It's who we are," said Sir Squirt.

"But look at my tail." Siona wiggled her tail before them. "I can help others with my tail. My tail is … is … helpful."

"Your tail is odd," he said.

Siona hung her head. "I'll try to be better. I'll try to make my tail less odd, but … but …"

"You'd be much better off losing that silly tail of yours and secreting your tunic," he said.

"That's right!" said Siona's mother. "Just look at this wondrous stuff."

Siona's mother tapped on Sir Squirt's bright blue tunic with one of her siphons. "Our tunics keep us safe and sound," she said, poking at her husband's tunic with a bit more force. "Without our tunics we would be eaten. That's why you have to stop swimming and grow up, my darling little larva."

"But," Siona said, wiggling her tail, "my tail can rescue—"

"Stop!" cried Sir Squirt. "And listen."

Siona stopped, holding her tail still.

A bubble rose from one of Sir Squirt's siphons, and he told her of the beauty and brilliance of the sea squirt strategy—that the grownups stayed put, but the young ones dispersed, finding new places to live, like settlers. Otherwise, there would be serious overcrowding. He demonstrated the capabilities of sea squirt siphons and took a long, deep drag with his left siphon, pulling in the sea and his lunch. He showed Siona how easy it was to grab a meal, not on the go but stuck to a rock. He waved his siphons, exclaiming that with all the energy saved in not fleeing from predators or chasing prey, there was much more energy left to make babies. He proudly declared that he and Siona's mother had made 985 larvae in their last brood. And lastly, he explained, as he patted his tunic with his siphons, that their very survival was due to the toughness of their cellulose tunics.

Siona cast a doubtful glance to his tunic. Dark translucent blue, it shimmered in the sunlight, casting light blue shadows onto the rock below. The strength of the tunic resided in special chemical bonds, or connections, between common molecules of sugar, all strung together to make bigger molecules—the mighty polysaccharides. The sugars were bound each to each with a beta 1,4 bond to make cellulose. But tweak that bond to the alpha 1,4 configuration and the outcome would be starch. With a simple switch in the chemical bonds, one could go from the indigestible bark of the redwood tree that would rise hundreds of feet above the forest floor, millions of years after this story takes place, to digestible mashed potatoes. And later, millions of years into the future, cellulose would become one of the most plentiful of biological polymers, found largely in plants—the presence of cellulose in sea squirts is a rare exception in the kingdom of animals. Siona brushed her tail across her mother's exceptionally smooth tunic.

"See?" said Siona's mother. "It's beautiful, isn't it?"

"And so strong!" said Sir Squirt, prodding his own tunic with great rigor. "Allow me to demonstrate." He poked himself again with his right siphon, triggering a gush of water from his left.

Siona bolted to the right to avoid the spurt of water. The surge of water knocked a nearby sea hare from the clump of red algae on which it was feeding. The animal landed without dignity on the floor of the tide pool in a puff of sand, tiny shells, and pebbles. Siona saw the creature pout, shake the sand from its back, and go right back to where it had been, as if it remembered exactly where it had taken its last bite.

Sir Squirt sighed, shaking his siphons. "Siona, the odds are not in your favor. Do you have any idea what your chances are? The probabilities that you will survive?"

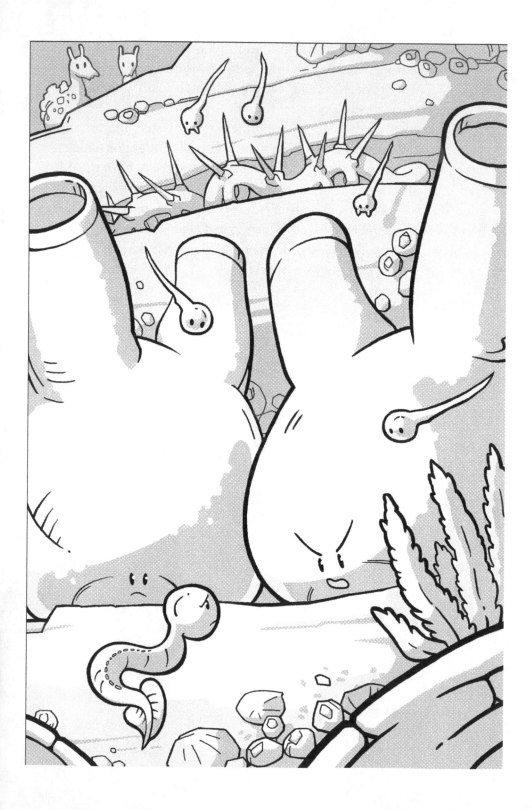

Siona shook her head.

"Only about 10 percent of you larvae will survive. Of the 985 of you, how many will survive? Do the math, Siona!"

So Siona did the math and multiplied 985 by 0.10, which equaled 98.5. She wasn't sure what to do with half a larva, but to be optimistic, she rounded up. Based on her calculations, the total number of surviving larvae would be ninety-nine. Ninety-nine of the larvae would survive and have children of their own. In turn, those would grow up and each have about ninety-nine surviving offspring of their own, and on and on it would go. She was sure her line would survive, even if she herself got lucky and found another way to live without growing up. She wanted to keep her tail.

A rotifer whirled overhead. "I'm sure glad that I don't have to stick my head to a rock," he declared, shrinking and expanding and twirling in the water.

Siona watched the rotifer twirl past. She sighed.

A second rotifer sailed past. "Show him what your widgets can do, Siona! Show him the beauty of your tail!"

Siona's eyes turned bright. She slapped the water with her tail. "My tail is not odd, and I'll beat the odds!" she cried. She whipped her tail, spinning like a top. "See?" she said. "Look at me! Look at my tail!"

The two adult sea squirts leaned back to avoid the whirling tail. They could not lean back far enough, and Siona's tail slammed into Sir Squirt's tunic, triggering a torrent of seawater from both siphons.

The spray landed squarely between the sharp spines of Helamite, a *Hallucigenia*, as he slept in the crack of a rock. He rose like a waking nightmare and stretched his fourteen clawed legs, shaking the seven pairs of long spines that ran down his back. Siona gasped, holding her tail still. Was she hallucinating? She stared back at the creature, her eyes wide.

"Do you mind?" said Helamite, blinking in the sunlight. "I am nocturnal and only wish to be awake at night."

"My apologies for the disruption, Helamite," said Sir Squirt sheepishly (even though sheep had not yet been domesticated from their wild Mouflon ancestors. The Mouflon also had not yet pranced on grassy plains, and the grasses had not yet sprouted and would not push their green spears through the soil for hundreds of millions of years after he made his sheepish comment).

Siona stared at the sharp spines, her tail rigid in the water.

"I was having a nightmare about this baby squirt who did not want to grow up. It was causing quite a ruckus." Helamite looked at Siona with bleary eyes. "I suspect that perhaps I was not dreaming. Is that correct?"

Siona could barely nod.

Helamite laughed, tapping his sharp spines together. They were hardened by the minerals of the sea, captured by his special protein widgets. With his spines he was well protected. A point he brought to Siona's attention when he stuck out one sharp spine and asked her to take a closer look. Siona touched the spine with her tail, and her eyes opened wide. Helamite turned in the water, pointing with a clawed foot to a Cambrian mussel, a clam, and a tiny shrimp, all nestled in a patch of lush green algae. The mussel and the clam had hard, strong shells. They, too, were clever biochemists, secreting special protein widgets that captured calcium and bicarbonate from the sea. Helamite pointed a long sharp spike at the tiny shrimp with its armored exoskeleton made from the mineralization of the polysaccharide chitin, enhanced with wee widgets cross-linked for extra strength and stiffness.

"Siona," said Sir Squirt, "our lifestyle is what keeps us alive. You do not have spiky things growing out of your body like Helamite, nor you do have a shell like a clam, nor are you equipped with the armor of a shrimp. Only your tunic will protect you. Siona, you need to grow up and grow up fast, or you will not survive."

Siona started to cry. "But I love my tail!"

Helamite looked at Siona and then back toward his sleeping spot in the dark, quiet crack in the rocks. He yawned. "Maybe there is hope, Siona. I have heard of a wise old clam and the Spanish dancer from afar. Maybe you can go find them in that faraway tide pool and get some help from those mollusks," said the creature, shaking his spines.

"Well, now," said Sir Squirt to the spiky creature, "that seems like quite a thought—suggesting that our little larva travel so far to change what we all know cannot be changed! I know she looks odd with that big tail of hers, but I say a sea squirt born, a sea squirt will be just that—a sea squirt! And there is not one clam, snail, shrimp, spider, sea star, sea hare, or proto-barnacle that is better or any different from the next. Who told you this nonsense?"

"My cousins who live in the same tide pool told me about the clam and the dancer long ago. I haven't spoken with them recently because they are an aggressive bunch, and they run around during the day when I'm *usually* sleeping." Helamite cast a second glance to his favorite crack in the dark rocks. "More recently, I heard the same thing from a ragworm. He arrived here after that last storm we had."

"A ragworm? A worm?" cried Sir Squirt in utter loathing. "An annelid, of all things!" he sputtered. "Never trust anything that a worm says. Don't you remember the stories of the ragworm and the pistol shrimp?" Sir Squirt covered his head with his siphons in exasperation.

"Of course I know the story of the ragworm and the pistol shrimp. We all know that story! First comes a cowardly ragworm," said Helamite, as if repeating a worn and tired tale, "and then comes a deadly pistol shrimp, ready to eat every sea squirt larva in range." The spiky creature paused, shaking his long, hard spines. Addressing Siona, Helamite continued, "The worm came to this tide pool from the sea, but there is a sea star named Sydney who knows of a secret passageway to the tide pool of Clarissa, the Clairvoyant Clam, and her friend the Spanish dancer. I strongly suggest that you find that star."

Sir Squirt pointed a siphon at Helamite. "Hold on a minute! That little star has been damaged beyond repair ever since he had that run-in with the pistol shrimp."

"It's such a pity," said Siona's mother. "That star was by far the fastest of all. And now there is no chance in heaven that he can survive." She sighed, her siphons dropping to the rock.

"And Siona," said Sir Squirt, "this is why you have to grow up. You need your tunic for protection. Your mother and I love all our little larvae, even you, with your big odd tail, but we cannot protect any of you. You need your tunic."

"Oh no," cried Siona. "I will be in a prison of cellulose without a tail!"

"Siona," said Sir Squirt in exasperation, "this is who we are. You cannot change what you are just because you want to become something else."

"But I'm more tail than anything else!" cried Siona. "My tail is who I am!"

Sir Squirt held his head with his siphons, squeezing out a couple of bubbles.

There was a jolt in the water. Siona felt the change in pressure, a hard push, and then a pull in the water. Screams rolled like waves through the tide pool. Instinctively, Siona dropped to the sandy floor below. Sir Squirt held Siona's mother in his siphons, and they both made shushing noises to the baby squirts that still lingered. A look of terror swept over Helamite, and the nightmarish creature crept off to hide in the rocks.

The supersonic bubbles pitted the sand like bullets. They came from the left, from around the bend of the black rock wall—the bend behind which Skinny, Blue, and Tiny had departed. Siona heard Tiny cry out and Skinny scream. Back around the bend raced Blue and a dozen others. They swam back to their parents, shaking. Siona raced to the rock wall, to the sound of screams pouring around the bend. There was another hail of bubbles. Caught in the turbulence, a wormlike creature slammed against the sandy bottom. It struggled with its twenty pairs of paddles to escape. Its fangs opened and closed, slicing through the water. The bubbles burst again, bombarding the creature, pushing it back across the sand. Another volley of bubbles sailed through the water, striking the open fangs. One fang twisted, and, struck by another round of the bubbles, it departed, leaving a gaping wound.

Siona heard Sir Squirt bellow. "It's a ragworm! No! No! Not the ragworm. The evil harbinger of death! Every time a ragworm appears, a deadly pistol shrimp is sure to follow."

Siona reached the rock wall. She peered around the corner. Little larvae fell like blue petals, their bodies littering the tide pool floor. Beneath the blanket of the dead, Tiny cringed under the shadow of the shrimp. The shrimp flicked his armored tail, stuffing his mouth, smacking. Bits and pieces sparkled in the sunlight, falling from the shrimp's mouth. The ragworm lay still in the sand, turning pale.

Siona wanted to cover her eyes with her tail. She could have turned away and swum away to safety with her strong, odd tail. Skinny screamed again. Siona saw him stuck, head down, on a red rock covered with stripes of green slime. *No, Skinny, no!* Siona cried to herself. The shrimp stopped munching. His gaze followed the sound of Skinny's cry.

With the shrimp distracted, Siona took a deep breath and plunged around the bend, racing to Tiny. She lifted Tiny with her tail. Above them, the shrimp towered, aiming his pistol claw at Skinny. Tiny shuddered, unable to move. Siona fled back to safety, carrying Tiny and dropping her behind the strong blue tunic of their mother.

Tiny blinked her eyes. "What about Skinny?" cried Tiny. But Siona was already gone, racing around the bend again.

Siona spied a pebble on the sandy bottom. She pushed her tail under the pebble and flung it as hard as she could. The pebble struck an outcropping of rock; the pistol shrimp turned, bombarding the rock with a volley of supersonic bubbles. Siona sped to Skinny, to the red rocks covered with green slime. This time she knew what to expect. She knew it would hurt; she knew it would burn. But she did it anyway. She did not have to urge Skinny to silence. He collapsed; his tail twitched once when it landed in a stripe of green slime. Siona worked her tail in a circle around Skinny's head. Tears filled her eyes. She jammed her tail under his head, silently calling on all of her widgets. With a flick of her tail, she forced Skinny free. He drifted to the bottom of the red rocks, burn marks on his head and tail. He could not move. She lifted him. He was heavy. Siona struggled to carry him. She thrashed in the water, making waves.

The shrimp turned. From the corner of her eye, Siona saw the shrimp take aim. She swam faster, beating her tail. The bend—safety—was close. All she needed was a few more seconds. Seconds. The seconds counted faster. The water swirled, not with deadly bubbles but with hundreds of rotifers.

"Use your widgets!" they cried to Siona. "Use your tail!" They sailed, twirling between Siona and the shrimp. Ball. Bat. Ball. Bat. The rotifers whirled everywhere, contracting to balls and expanding to bats. The shrimp balked, flicking his tail and swatting at the rotifers with his claws, giving Siona and Skinny the seconds that they needed.

A second chance. A hail of burning bubbles exploded behind them as they escaped around the bend.

Siona called for help.

"What did you do this time?" cried Blue, streaking to her with half a dozen other larvae, including Tiny.

"He's hurt," cried Siona, panting, as she lowered Skinny to the tide pool floor. "He got burned by the green slime on the red rocks."

"Not that excuse again!" screamed Blue, and he almost hit Siona with his tail. "Go away! You don't belong here. You're a menace!" He turned to his brother, touching Skinny's damaged head and tail to apply the lifesaving nanoscale whiskers and special cellulose blend.

"But … but …" sobbed Siona, her tail burning. "It wasn't my fault. I … I …" She swallowed and hung her head.

Tiny beat the water with her tail. "Siona is telling the truth! She rescued Skinny from the green slime *and* the pistol shrimp!"

"Oh, you are telling big tales now," said Blue. "There is no such thing as green slime, and no sea squirt larva can survive a direct hit from a pistol shrimp. You saw it all wrong with those little eyes of yours!"

"I know what I know," insisted Tiny. She swam to Siona and covered the burned area of Siona's tail with bright blue nanoscale whiskers. "I know what I know," she whispered again to Siona.

Siona turned to take a look at her tail; the burn marks were disappearing. "Thank you," she whispered back.

"You got it all wrong again, Siona," said Tiny. "We should be the ones to thank you." But before she could continue to argue her point, Sir Squirt began to bellow.

"See, see!" cried Sir Squirt from his rock. "This is why you need to grow up! This is why you need your tunic! There is nothing you can do to stop the pistol shrimp!"

"More than ever it's time to grow up," cried Siona's mother to the larvae, waving her siphons. "Find a lovely rock!"

In reply, Siona heard the other larvae sing back, chanting, as they swam from their hiding places.

> Find a rock
> Find a rock,

On which to dock
On which to grow.
This is all we need to know.

Even Tiny sang the song; the words and the melody came so naturally.

Skinny rose from the tide pool floor. He swam past Siona, not saying a word, and joined the others, each of whom were intent on finding the perfect rock. Siona hovered in the water, alone. Even Tiny was gone. She looked back at her tail. In the shadow it was sapphire blue. A tunic of cellulose might be one way to survive, but a big strong tail had its merits too. Siona took a deep breath and swam to her mother and Sir Squirt.

"Goodbye," she said, touching them with the tip of her head. "I don't belong here, and I have to find out why." And off she swam, seeking a clairvoyant clam and the lovely Spanish dancer, with her tail making waves behind her.

*   *   *

"**W**ait!" cried Siona the human, jumping from the rocking chair, her face pale. "Siona should stay in her tide pool where she can be safe! She needs her tunic! What will happen if she runs into another pistol shrimp?" Siona paced across the carpet. "The ocean is so big. What if some giant wave catches her and throws her into the ocean? What would happen to Siona in all that water? Siona is such a little squirt, and there is so much water in the ocean!"

"There is," replied her mother.

"How many gallons of water are there in the sea?" Siona asked. Her hands shaking, she bit her lip.

"There are about 352 point 670 quintillion gallons of water in all the oceans." Siona's mother picked up a pad of paper and pen from the end table. "We can write that down as 352,670,000,000,000,000,000 or 3.5267 times ten raised to the power of twenty." She handed the pad of paper to Siona. "Can you imagine all the gallon milk cartons you would need to fill the oceans?"

Siona shook her head and shuddered, her shoulders rounded. She took her seat on the rocking chair and stared up at the ceiling, clutching the pad of paper.

Siona's mother got up from the chair and picked up an old vinyl record. She placed it on the turntable, and it began to spin. The turntable was so old that even Siona's babysitter had never seen one before. Siona's mother dropped the needle down and returned to the rocking chair to take her seat by her daughter. Siona started to draw as the song started.

It was a recording made long ago by Siona's father, before the wrinkles around his eyes became permanent fixtures. *Scratch, scratch,* the record played, rising and falling in a whisper. From a piano, the first four notes played a simple melody. The sequence of the notes changed, first one pattern and then another. The four notes transformed to four chords. A guitar joined in. A trumpet sang, drums pounded, and a flute whistled. A medley of strings entered, and the song took off on an explosion of its own. With the vocals it was as if the entirety of all creation joined in, reaching for the crescendo. The song surged and then paused. Beats went past in silence, and then the first four notes played again, repeating, quieting, until the only sound was the *scratch, scratch* of the needle on the record. Siona's mother got up and lifted the needle and carefully returned it to its stand.

Siona was still drawing, pressing the pen hard against the paper. She swallowed, the color drained from her face. Her breathe came in short, tight little gasps.

"Are you all right?" asked her mother.

"Here," Siona said, handing her mother the pad of paper.

Siona's mother sat down on the rocking chair and took the pad of paper. On the paper a dark wave rose to a point over a figure standing on a rock littered with fossils. The feet of the figure were nothing but bones etched into the rock below, becoming fossils themselves. "Oh," said Siona's mother, "I can't believe it!" She pointed to one of the fossils in the picture. "Is that a *Dickinsonia costata?*"

Siona sighed.

Her mother looked up from the drawing. "It is, isn't it?" asked her mother.

Siona sighed again. "Yes, Mom. That's exactly what it is."

"And it's a lovely example of one too," said her mother, looking back down at the picture. "You're a great illustrator."

Siona looked down at the bandage that covered her middle finger.

Her mother moved closer, and she brushed Siona's hair back from the curve of her cheek. "Do you have any questions that I could answer?"

"Any questions?" asked Siona, twisting a lock of hair around her forefinger so tight that the tip of her finger turned red.

"Something that needs to be answered?"

"Oh, a question that needs an answer. I get it now," said Siona. She looked up at the ceiling, her lips pressed together. She turned back to her mother, "Why does that little creature Propikaia have such a long name?" she asked.

"That was *Primogenitus notochordus-neotenous*, and that is the imaginary name of an imaginary creature. I made up the name so I could tell you our story."

Siona brought the palm of her hand to her forehead.

Her mother laughed. "Siona, this story is fictitiously factual, or perhaps it is factually fictitious."

"But why such long crazy names that are so hard to say? What do they mean?" asked Siona.

"We all have some long crazy names," said her mother. "And they do mean something."

"I have some long, crazy, hard-to-say names too? Me?"

Siona's mother nodded and picked up a pen and the pad of paper with Siona's drawing from the end table. And Siona's mother wrote the following:

Kingdom: Animalia
Phylum: Chordata
Class: Mammalia
Order: Primates
Family: Hominiodea
Genus: Homo
Species: sapiens

"Those are your names," said Siona's mother showing her daughter the list. And she underlined the words "Phylum: Chordata."

"And the Spanish dancer?" asked Siona. "Do I have the same names as the Spanish dancer?"

"The Spanish dancer in this story is not a dancer from Spain. The Spanish dancer is a mollusk, like a clam, octopus, snail, or slug. In fact, the Spanish dancers today are like slugs."

"Oh," said Siona, "so the Spanish dancer in this story is like a beautiful swimming slug wearing a bright red frilly dress." She sighed. "It's too bad that the name mollusk does not sound very pretty."

Siona's mother laughed. "About eighty thousand different types of creatures have been assigned to the phylum of Mollusca."

"What? What do you mean by the word *phlegm*?"

"No, the word is p-h-y-l-u-m, not phlegm." Siona's mother turned to a new page on the pad of paper. "If we were to classify our Cambrian Spanish dancer, we might see something like this." And Siona's mother wrote the following:

Kingdom: Animalia
Phylum: Mollusca
Class: Gastropoda
Order: Protonudibranchia
Family: Neohexabranchidae
Genus: ?
Species: ?

"But what about the ragworm that bit me today?" questioned Siona. "Is a ragworm a mollusk too?"

"No, a ragworm is an annelid, like an earthworm. The ragworm that you met today has segments too. If we were to classify the ragworm, we could use the following," and she wrote:

Kingdom: Animalia
Phylum: Annelida

Class: Polychaeta
Order: Aciculata
Family: Nereidae
Genus: Nereis
Species: virens

"What about Sydney the Star? Is he either a mollusk or an annelid?" asked Siona.

"A sea star is an echinoderm or creature with a radial symmetry. If a scientist were to classify Sydney the Sea Star, the classification might look something like this." And Siona's mother wrote:

Kingdom: Animalia
Phylum: Echinodermata
Class: Asteroidea
Order: Primoforcipulatida
Family: Preasteriidae
Genus: ?
Species: ?

"And Siona the Sea Squirt? What about her classification?"

Siona's mother smiled and wrote, underlining the words "Phylum: Chordata" again:

Kingdom: Animalia
Phylum: Chordata
Class: Protoascidiacea
Order: Preenterogona
Family: Propikaicionidae
Genus: Cionagracilens
Species: ?

"Hey," said Siona, picking up the pad of paper and flipping to the page with her classification. She pointed to the word "Chordata." She flipped the pages forward and pointed to the same word in Siona's classification. "Siona the Sea Squirt and I are in the same club. We're in the same phlegm! How can that be?"

4

Glass Spicules, Zinc, and Ink

Siona set out, with sweeping strokes of her tail, to find where she belonged. Swimming backward, she took in the final view of her nursery. She waved goodbye with her tail and sailed around the bend to the right, her nursery gone from view. It took a simple flick of her tail to switch from swimming backward to swimming forward. She smiled at the dexterity of her tail until she collided with a wall. Tiny pores covered the wall, like minute windows. Her head was sucked inside a dark chamber through one of the pores, while her tail wiggled on the outside. Thin rays of light poked through the lattice of the pores, crisscrossing the chamber. She tried to pull free, but the right side of her head was glued to the inside of the chamber by some sticky stuff. Three tiny spicules of glass, sharp as daggers, held her in place. She winced. Between the glass and the glue, Siona was stuck.

Thousands of whiplike flagella churned the water inside the chamber. They danced and waved, their microtubule widgets a marvel of nature. With mechanical prowess, the monstrous primordial flagella beat the left side of Siona's head silly. The water inside the chamber turned to a torrent. Above the chamber, Siona saw a circle of blue through a narrow opening. There was a chance. Freedom was there, just above. If only she could make it through the opening. She tried again to wiggle free, but the glue held her head fast, and the glass spicules jabbed into her body. *Slap-slap* went the flagella.

"Ouch," cried Siona. "What did I get myself into this time?"

"A sponge," cried the creature, its voice reverberating in the dark chamber, "the lowest of all animals! You probably thought I wasn't even an animal at all!" The sponge laughed. "I caught you, and I can't even move!"

Siona cringed at the sound of the sponge. With all the power she could muster, she began to whip the tip of her tail counterclockwise. Her body began to corkscrew through the pore; her head still was held by the glue. There was a pop as her tail squeezed through the pore. And into the depths of the cavernous sponge went the rest of Siona. Glued by her head, Siona grappled with the monstrous flagella beating her tail.

"I'm stuck by my head," cried Siona in disbelief. "And I'm not even ready to grow up!" The laughter of the sponge echoed in the chamber. At least now the glass spicules no longer jabbed her body. She looked up at the ring of bright blue above. In the circle of blue, Siona saw Skinny swim overhead.

The beating of the flagella inside the sponge synchronized, beating in unison and forcing her slowly down. After millions of years of development, the proficiency of the flagella was not surprising. Millions of years before Siona's time, countless protozoa and single-celled creatures had used these structures like tiny oars to propel themselves through the water. In the case of the sponge, there was a slight modification. Rather than moving the sponge through the water, the flagella moved the water through the sponge, aiding in the capture of food, which included the occasional sea squirt larva. At the base of the sponge, Siona noted a black fluid. It did not smell good. The flagella were pushing her down closer to the black pit.

Above the beating of the flagella, Siona heard Sir Squirt scream, "Oh no! Oh no! Not that evil thing! Not again! Swim, children, swim!" His voice carried well in the water, even around the bend. "Hide in the rocks; secrete your tunics now!" The flagella continued to push Siona downward.

Through a pore in the sponge wall, she managed to look out. Sea squirt larvae darted in all directions. She heard them scream. "No, no!" they cried. "Not another ragworm!"

The flagella continued to beat. Her downward journey brought her to another pore. On the other side, Siona caught a glimpse of a monster.

Bright brilliant yellow, a single eye from the monster peered in at her. Below the single eye was a pair of gleaming fangs. Siona thought it might be best to stay in the sponge. But inside the sponge it grew darker, and the dark fluid at the base swirled as if in anticipation. Siona fought. She wiggled. The glue held her head even as she descended. She tried to slow her downward descent by sticking her tail out of another pore, but she was jabbed by sharp spicules. She pulled her tail back into the sponge.

Above the cries of the squirts and the beating of flagella, there came a voice. "Hello, Siona. How are you?"

"Well, I'm doing okay. Thank you for asking," said Siona. "But I would like to get out of this sponge if possible."

"Maybe I can help," said the voice.

Siona heard Sir Squirt yell something about a ragworm and that she should not listen. "Evil, evil!" Sir Squirt bellowed from around the bend.

"How fast are you moving down?" asked the voice.

"I think I'm moving down at about one centimeter per minute. That's my best estimation," said Siona.

"And how far away are you from the black bottom of the sponge?"

"Hmm," said Siona. "I estimate that I'm about seven centimeters away."

Siona thought she heard something like a cough. "Do the math, Siona, and calculate how much time before you di—before you reach the black base of the sponge."

"Oh, that's easy," said Siona. "The time would equal the distance divided by the speed. So that would be seven centimeters divided by one centimeter per minute, which equals seven minutes," she said with pride.

"Good. That gives us some time. And is your tail still free?"

Careful to avoid the glass spicules, Siona stuck the tip of her tail through a pore. She wiggled her tail for a few short seconds, still unsure which was worse—the sponge or the yellow monster.

"All right," said the voice. "That's good, that's good. We have a chance." And then the voice went silent. Siona waited as the flagella pushed her down and down.

"So," said Siona, trying to free herself from the sticky stuff of the sponge, "I was wondering if you have any ideas." She was getting closer to the black fluid, and the odor was unpleasant.

"You will need to do two things," said the voice. "First, you need to reverse the beating of the flagella. Right now you are still moving down. Is that right?"

"Yes," said Siona, "that's right."

"Okay," said the voice, "you can reverse the flagella by hitting the sponge with your tail as hard as you can and in as many places as you can. That way the sponge will feel that you are too big to be digested and will try to force you back out."

"*Digested?*" cried Siona, sliding closer to the dark pit below. She heard the sea squirt larvae sing as they swam past the sponge. The sponge and its other inhabitants responded to the song. Light flashed, coursing from bioluminescent bacteria to the fiber optic glass spicules of the sponge. The sponge turned into a strobe light. Siona blinked in the pulsing light.

"You need to start in one minute," said the voice. "I'll count it down for you. Once the flagella stop moving, you will need to use some scissors to cut through the glue before the flagella reverse direction."

"Scissors! I don't have any scissors!" said Siona, trying hard not to panic in the pulsing light.

"That black material at the bottom of the sponge contains little widgets that are like scissors or proteases. You need to scoop up the scissors with your tail and apply them only to the glue that is holding your head. Don't touch the scissors to your head, and be prepared for your tail to burn."

"*What?*" cried Siona, not quite understanding the chemical capabilities of a sponge, that even without decades of training from textbooks like *Palladium-catalyzed Cross Coupling in the Organic Synthesis of Complex Molecules*, the primordial sponge, a clever biochemist, had no problem making widgets of glue, glass, and even scissors.

"I'm going to start counting down now, Siona. Get ready. Five, four, three, two, one, now! Siona, now!"

Siona started thrashing her tail, striking as hard as she could against the inner wall of the sponge. Bam, bam, bam!

"Keep going, keep going!" cried the voice.

She beat the innards of the sponge, whipping her tail like the flagella. Some of the glue from the sponge wall stuck to her tail, forming a protective barrier. For a moment, her tail stuck to the glue of the sponge, but she wrenched her tail free. The flagella stopped beating. Siona panted. She was close to the noxious black liquid. She dipped her tail in the black fluid, scooped up the scissor widgets, and spread them over the glue holding her head. The tip of her tail began to burn. She cried. She dipped her tail again to add more of the black goo to the glue. She felt the glue loosen. She thrashed. She twisted. She fought. She shook her head. She was free!

The flagella reversed their beating. The flow of water raged up through the sponge in a torrent, carrying debris, diatoms, and a lone rotifer in its wake—and Siona. She shot out of the orifice of the sponge like a rocket bursting from a silo. She headed straight toward a sharp overhanging rock. Siona closed her eyes and braced for the impact. There was a swish of brilliant yellow and fangs glinted, followed by a collective scream from the sea squirts. The fangs opened. Siona saw her dreams severed before her eyes. *I'll never swim again*, she thought. The fangs closed down on her fragile body, stopping her headlong flight to the overhanging rock, holding her gently, carrying her down, and releasing her to the safety of the tide pool floor. When the monster opened his fangs to speak, it was with the same voice that had guided Siona from the sponge.

"Well done, Siona!" said the voice in the body of a fang-bearing, brilliant, bright, yellow monster of a ragworm.

Siona slipped into unconsciousness.

The ragworm lifted Siona, cradling her in his fangs. He paddled to a tiny larva. He motioned to Siona's damaged tail with his fangs, whispering of the healing powers of nanoscale whiskers and special cellulose blend.

The larva nodded, keeping her eyes focused on the fangs. It was Tiny. She touched Siona's tail with her head, transferring the nanoscale whiskers. "Now we are even," whispered Tiny, and she turned to the worm. "You're a different kind of worm, aren't you?"

In reply, the ragworm nodded, his fangs luminous.

Tiny glanced at the fangs, flicked her tail, gave Siona a kiss, and departed into a forest of algae.

Siona stirred in the sand. She opened her eyes. The fangs above her came into sharp focus. She blinked, wiggling her tail. Her tail felt much better. In the gleam of the fangs, Siona saw her reflection, a tiny being of head and tail. She gulped. The great creature bent his head, and her image slipped from the fangs.

On the squirt's shiny body, the worm's reflection looked back at him. His fangs opened and closed, arching into a half smile. The mighty worm shook his head; the reflection did the same. He turned to go.

Siona rose from the sandy floor. "Wait! Wait!" she cried after the worm.

He stopped, turning to face the squirt.

Siona stared along the length of the beast before her, the twenty segments brilliant yellow in the sun. Each segment was lined with two paddles on each side. And then there were the fangs. Siona swallowed.

"I … I … want to thank you," she whispered.

"You are welcome," said the worm.

Siona paused and then bowed deeply, which was really more like sticking her head into the sand. "Thank you for saving me," Siona said again.

The worm nodded and turned to leave.

"Wait!" cried Siona again, swimming after the great creature and coming alongside. "So why did you?"

"Why did I what?" asked the worm.

"Save me."

"Oh, I didn't save you. You saved yourself. I just gave you a little coaching, that's all." The worm smiled, his fangs arching.

Siona blinked and looked away from the fangs into the deep eyes of the worm. "Why did you? Why did you coach me?"

"I guess because I thought I could," replied the worm.

"And you always do things just because you can?" asked Siona.

"I suppose so."

"Is there anything you cannot do?"

"Well, yes, of course. All living things have their limitations."

"Well, what is your limitation?" Siona asked.

"Oh, I have my limitations all right."

"Prove it," said Siona.

The ragworm laughed. "I think you have that a bit backward. Normally, one has to prove what one can do and not what one cannot."

"Well, maybe I am not your normal sea squirt larva."

"That may be. Maybe I am not your normal ragworm."

"That may be. So … what can a non-normal ragworm not do?"

The ragworm hesitated. Siona swam closer to the worm in encouragement, temporarily ignoring the mighty fangs.

"I cannot swim in an inside-out, upside-down circle," said the worm. His paddles drooped, and he brushed the sand with his fangs, making two parallel tracks.

"And that is important to you?" Siona asked.

"Yes."

"Why?"

"Because."

"Because then you could?"

"Yes."

"What does an inside-out, upside-down circle look like? Maybe I can try."

"Well, first, you gain some speed. You swim as fast as you can go, diving down, and then you pull up and up and up, going upside down and backward, making a circle and coming back to where you have just been."

"That seems like a lot of effort to get to where you already are," said Siona, thinking out loud as she wiggled forward. She dove deep and then rushed up and up into a near-perfect back loop. With that effort, she ended up exactly where she had been. "You mean like that?"

"Yes, like that," cried the ragworm in surprise. "That's some tail you have!"

"Why don't you give it a try?"

"I am not designed for that kind of maneuver."

Siona looked earnestly at the worm. "You saved me from a sponge. In my humble opinion, I think you can do anything. Maybe you need some coaching."

"Okay, what should I do?" asked the worm.

"Start as fast as you can go, dive way down, then go straight up, arch your back, and complete the circle. In other words, paddle like heck!"

The ragworm smiled. He paddled, diving down.

"Great job!" cried Siona.

He paddled straight up.

"Great job!" repeated Siona.

He went into an arch, paddling upside down and backward. He began the descent like a torpedo, his fangs opened wide and horrible. Siona cringed. The worm's fangs snapped shut with an explosive bang. Siona gasped. The worm's paddles caught his own turbulence, and he tumbled out of control, twisting and falling. His fangs hit the sand while his body still corkscrewed. He was buried in the sand up to his fifth segment before he came to a stop.

"Wow. Very, very good! And very dramatic with that fang snap of yours! I bet you could cut right through rock with those fangs," cried Siona. "That was a great effort for the first time!"

The ragworm yanked himself from the ground, flinging sand every which way. There was no way that Siona could have ever guessed how many times he had attempted the inside-out, upside-down circle. In fact, it was a maneuver all worms were driven to attempt. At the apex of the circle, the fangs of a ragworm could open wider than at any other time. With the fangs opened that wide, they could snap shut with great force. It was at that point that ragworm fangs were their most lethal. Unfortunately, no worm had ever completely mastered the inside-out, upside-down circle.

"That was amazing!" cried Siona, thumping her tail. "I even got goose bumps! With a bit of practice you'll do even better!"

The ragworm smiled at the young squirt. But there was no way that Siona could possibly get goose bumps, no matter how excited she was when the ragworm's fangs snapped shut. She would have to be an animal with hair or fur, and that wouldn't happen on the planet for an estimated 396 million years after this story takes place.

"Well, thank you for the coaching," he said. "I think we should introduce ourselves formally," said the worm. "Generally, my phylum and yours should never be seen together."

"Oh, that seems silly," said Siona with a tiny huff.

"It goes way back, through generations."

"Well, I am a new generation, and I say we change all that bad stuff to good stuff."

"Very well, young squirt. Please tell me your name."

"Siona."

"I thought so," said the worm. "Rumors in the tide pool do move quickly. You know how fast and far sound travels in water, don't you?"

Siona shook her head. She did not know that the sound of her own voice traveled through the sea at 1,560 meters per second (3,438.6 miles per hour), nearly five times faster than the speed of sound in air.

"Yes," said the ragworm, "the talk of the tide pool is that there is a little sea squirt larva who does not want to grow up. It seems to me that you might be that little squirt."

"When I swim I can feel the water molecules stroke my tail," said Siona, swimming a circle around the worm. "I feel like I'm meant to swim forever. I think I must be the only squirt in the whole tide pool that feels this way."

"There is nothing wrong with being different," said the worm.

"I don't want to grow up if it means sticking my head to a rock for the rest of my life. It was bad enough being stuck in that sponge." She swam another inside-out, upside-down circle, ending right in front of the ragworm, though careful to avoid the fangs.

The ragworm glanced at her with a mixture of amusement, envy, and awe. "How do you plan on doing that, on changing your future?"

"I'm not sure, but there must be a way, just like you will be able to swim an inside-out, upside-down circle someday."

Had the ragworm had eyebrows, he would have raised them, as they are excellent tools in nonverbal communication. But the appearance of eyebrows would have to wait for the arrival of a nearly hairless hominin, about 521 million years after this story takes place. In the absence of eyebrows, the ragworm simply nodded, with his fangs gleaming in the sun.

Siona winced at the fangs but held her position in the water. "Mr. Ragworm, I don't want to stick my head to a rock forever and ever," she whispered.

The ragworm leaned forward, and with his brutal fangs, he gently touched Siona right above her eyespots on what might have been her forehead, if she should have had one. Siona looked into worm's eyes. Her own reflection stared back.

"You can call me N. Reilly Zincfangness, or Reilly Z., or Reilly for short," said the worm.

Siona looked up at the brilliant yellow worm. He smiled ruefully, clicking fangs hardened by zinc from the sea and rich in specialized fibrous protein widgets called ragworm fang proteins (RFPs). With what nature gave the worm naturally, he had no need of metal smelting.

"Siona," said the worm, his voice barely above a whisper, "it takes courage to accept what will be."

Siona hesitated. With a defiant flip of her tail, she cried, "It takes courage to be ... to be ... a ..."

"Yes," interrupted Reilly the Ragworm, "it does take courage to be."

A rotifer swam past. "Courage is a widget! Courage is a widget!" it cried.

"Come with me," cried Siona to the worm. "We can be explorers together and find Clarissa the Clairvoyant Clam and her friend the lovely Spanish dancer, so I can swim forever, and you can swim a perfect inside-out, upside-down circle!"

"Siona," said the worm, "remember your phylum and mine should not be seen together."

"Not that again! You already said that, and I think it is plain silly. We can be renegades with the courage to make our own plans and certainly our own friends!" She made a whoosh with her tail for emphasis.

Reilly's paddles drooped. He rubbed his fangs along the sand, making two parallel tracks, and sighed. Siona held her tail as still as she could. "I think you should know about what happened. I will not go with you until you give me the chance to tell you the truth," said Reilly.

"The truth? Do we know what that is?" asked Siona.

"Since before I was hatched, there have been bitter times between ragworms and sea squirts."

"Is that the truth?" asked Siona.

"Yes, a long, long, long time ago a ragworm tried to catch a shrimp.

Mind you, this was no ordinary shrimp. It was a fearsome pistol shrimp that could blast the largest snail right out of its shell."

"Blast a snail right out of its shell?" repeated Siona. She thought back to the blasting of bubbles and the terrified shrieks of the sea squirt larvae earlier that day.

"Yes, with its supersonic bubbles," continued Reilly. "A long time ago, my grandfather's great-great-grandfather tried to catch such a shrimp, but his fangs were not strong enough to cut through the shrimp's armor."

"You mean he tried to catch the pistol shrimp in his fangs?"

"Yes," said Reilly. "He wanted to cut the pistol claw from the shrimp before ... before ..."

The two animals hovered together in silence.

"Do we need to know what happened in the past?" whispered Siona.

Reilly nodded. His fangs opened and shut. "The shrimp tried to kill the worm. He had his pistol claw aimed right at the worm. But as the supersonic bubbles burst from that hideous claw, the worm dove."

"So what could be so bad about that? The worm made the right decision," said Siona.

"They were there too."

"Who was there?"

"The baby sea squirts—hundreds of them, hatching from their eggs."

"Oh no!"

"The bubbles hit the squirts. Had the worm held his position, maybe some of them would have lived."

"Were they all lost? The entire brood?"

"Yes, all of them. Gone." The worm hung his head; his fangs brushed the sand. "Now you know the whole story. You know the truth."

Siona was quiet. She looked into the fierce face of the worm.

"Do I? Does anyone really know the whole story? We weren't there. Maybe there was another reason why your grandfather's great-great-grandfather dove down so deep. Did anyone ever ask him? That dive ... isn't that the first part of an inside-out, upside-down circle? Maybe the storytellers got the story all wrong."

The worm and the squirt floated above the tide pool floor.

The worm clicked his fangs together. "I would be honored to join you as a fellow explorer in your quest for Clarissa the Clam and her friend the Spanish dancer," he said, with a smile that parted his fangs into a perfect arch.

"Oh, thank you! Thank you," cried Siona. "Let's get going right now!"

The water swirled. There was a whoosh as a brown blob-like thing of a creature landed between them. A cloud of purple ink rose from the back of the creature. Reilly tried to push Siona away from the cloud with his great fangs.

"Swim, Siona! Swim!" the ragworm cried.

Beyond the purple veil of ink, Siona could barely make out a strange-looking lump with two big earlike appendages. Dots and circles covered its squishy body. Siona felt confused and dizzy. The walls of the tide pool spun and tilted.

"I feel so sleepy, and it looks like such a lovely place for a nap," said Siona, closing her eyes.

"*No!* Wake up, Siona!" cried Reilly.

But it was too late. She was dreaming even before she landed on the bottom of the tide pool. She saw herself swimming with a strong tail in a sunlit sea. Her tail whipped from side to side, forming ripples as she sped ahead. She dove down and looked back. She saw the blue tunics of her mother and her grandparents and their grandparents' parents, and all her squirt ancestors stretching back as far as she could see. Their siphons moved with the currents. They seemed to be waving goodbye. To be polite, Siona waved goodbye with her strong tail and then turned, swimming away from the squirts. *I must have grown up without sticking my head to a rock*, dreamed Siona. Before her, at the edge of the sea, she saw a strange creature standing tall on two sturdy and long appendages, waving two more appendages above. *Those are not siphons*, thought Siona. The creature's cloth tunic was bright white.

Spying Siona in the sea, the strange creature smiled. "Hello, hello! You are my sister. My name is Siona too!"

Siona had no idea how they could be sisters. She looked up through the ripples of the water at the other Siona. Another similar creature joined the other Siona on the shore. He, too, walked on tall, sturdy, long appendages. "Siona, Siona," he called, introducing himself as Aristotle. "I was the first to classify the sea squirts one fine summer day in the year 342 BC. I called you all mollusks, but I was wrong."

"That's a good thing," said the earthbound Siona, "because the word *mollusk* does not suit such a beautiful creature."

The earthbound Siona leaned down, touching the water with five delicate fingers, almost like a five-pointed star. The five fingers wiggled in the water. One stroked Siona from her head to the tip of her tail. Siona felt a tap, tap on her tail.

"**O**h, I am so, so sorry," cried the blob-like creature. "Maybe if you gave her another tap with your fangs, she might wake up. I am so sorry to be such trouble." The blob-like creature shook his head, swishing the water with what looked like two large ears. "It's all my fault," he sobbed.

Siona stirred on the tide pool floor. She blinked her eyes. The tide pool spun. She closed her eyes; the world still rotating.

"Siona, Siona, it's okay now. The ink is gone," said the worm.

"The ink?" said Siona, opening her eyes again. She tried to focus on the blob-like creature, but dots and circles roamed at will across the creature's squishy body. Siona turned to look away. Red and green algae swept slowly with the rhythm of the sea. Limpet-like creatures clung to rock walls in their green shelly tipis. A cluster of blue-lipped proto-barnacles, with orange and red feelers, languidly stroked the water. A pair of polychaete worms, dressed in yellow lace, chased a velvet worm into a burrow. Creatures with long, thin stalks rose above the tide pool floor like a bouquet of flowers, their crown of tentacles the petals of a tulip. The story of life had began to write its own history, its characters chiseled into fossilized tablets of stone, like the pages of a beautifully written old book. Some pages of that history would be lost with the duration of time. Some never to be found; such was the rarity of the characters. Yet all the pages, written in the language of life, translated into a pure and universal tongue of only four letters—the enduring language of past, present, and future.

"It is all so beautiful and perfect," Siona murmured, turning back to the circles and dots of the blob-like creature.

"Oh! I'm beautiful and perfect?" cried the blob-like creature. "No one has ever paid me such a compliment before!"

Above Siona, a pair of creatures twirled in their spiraled shells; their tentacles intertwined. They were so rare they never would be found in the fossil record.

"So lovely, so lovely," cried Siona.

"I'm lovely? Me? Lovely?" cried the blob-like creature.

The ten orange arms of two stalked echinoderms waved like the fronds of palm trees.

"Miraculous!" cried Siona. "So … so … special!"

"Oh, you are too kind! Too kind!" cried the blob-like creature.

Siona stared at the blob-like creature, and it snapped into focus. It was a common sea hare. The crazy-looking structures on top of its head bobbed up and down as he nodded.

"Oh, I didn't mean y—" Siona saw the flicker of a smile begin to fade. She shook her head. "Oh yes! You are one of the most special creatures I have ever seen in this entire tide pool."

"I am? Me?" asked the sea hare. "You look special too. I've never seen a larva with such a big tail."

Siona looked back at her tail. She saw Reilly close his fangs, and the worm's fierce face softened into a faint smile. She smiled back, but as a lone passing cloud plunged the tide pool into gloom, the worm opened his dreaded fangs, and his smile disappeared. He glanced in the direction from which the hare had arrived. The purple ink had dissipated. But its signal still lingered, a biological flag of warning—a black skull and crossbones on a background of yellow. Advancing in the wake of the wind, the cloud moved past the sun, and brightness returned to the tide pool.

"Why, I thought I looked like all the other sea hares," continued the hare. "There must be hundreds of us all with the same dots and circles, all in the exact same places. I never ever felt special before."

"Oh no, you are quite special. And you have those lovely things on your head that wave back and forth in a special way. What are those things on top of your head?"

"As far as I know, all of my relatives have the same things, and they look exactly the same. They are my rhinophores. Do you like them? Do you think they look special?"

"Oh, you have the loveliest rhinopharts I have ever seen," said Siona.

"Um, they are called rhinophores, not rhinopharts," corrected the sea hare.

"Oh, yes! Rhinophores!" said Siona, shaking her head as if that might shake off the effects of the ink. "What do they do, those rhinophores of yours?"

"They are my olfactory sensors, and they help me find stuff by smell." And as if to demonstrate the keen capabilities of his rhinophores, he pointed them right at Siona. His rhinophores twitched; he twitched. The molecules of scent from Siona's new young life bound with great tenacity to receptors deep within the hare's rhinophores. The hare assumed a look of bliss.

"Wow," said Siona as enthusiastically as she could, especially considering that she had been unconscious moments before. She beat her tail, lifting up from the sand so she could peer into the rhinophores. Inside the tapered structures, grooves and ridges crisscrossed. Ordered lines of pores, like little windows, opened and closed in sequence. Clusters of colored cilia fanned the water above each pore. "Those rhinopharts … rhinophores sure are special!" cried Siona.

"Why, thank you! And your friend, the worm, has a most unusal scent, like metal and courage." The hare swung his rhinophores toward Reilly. He seemed to take a deep breath through his rhinophores. "Very unusual scent," he repeated. "Once I learn a scent, I never forget it. I remember it forever and ever," said the hare.

"That is so facinating … and special!" said Siona.

"Really? Do you think so?" asked the hare.

"Absolutely. You are a model organism of learning and memory," said Siona.

"Well, what about my purple ink? Do you think it's special too? It's been a trademark of my family for eons. It squirts right out my backside when I'm scared, like a smoke screen and decoy at the same time. It protects me," said the hare. Pointing to Siona and Reilly with his left rhinophore, he added, "And other creatures too."

"That ink of yours is some pretty nasty stuff," interjected Reilly, fidgeting as he scanned the tide pool. The rhinophores of the sea hare, which moments before had been standing upright, suddenly drooped.

"But it is especially nasty stuff!" cried Siona. "That ink of yours is really unique; it's a great trick!"

"Do you think so?" asked the hare.

"Yes, of course," said Siona. "And I bet you have a special name too."

"You want to know my name?" asked the hare, his rhinophores on the rise.

Siona nodded.

"It's Harold," whispered the hare.

"What a special name!" said Siona.

The hare beamed. His rhinophores swayed above his head, making circles. He leaned closer to Siona and the ragworm, whispering, "But … but please, be careful. There are some terrible, nasty creatures in these waters." He glanced back, his rhinophores trembling. "Those pistol shrimp mean trouble for a young squirt like you," said Harold to Siona. "But nothing is more dreadful than the purple sea spiders. They can rip the arms right off a sea star and even the fangs from a lesser worm than you." The hare pointed a rhinophore at Reilly. "And today, right before we were introduced, I saw the biggest and nastiest sea spider I have ever, ever seen."

The sea hare's squishy body suddenly tightened. There was an eerie ripple in the water above. From an outcropping of rock, a single, four-jointed, dark purple leg emerged. Sharp spines stuck out from the tough exoskeleton. The leg, ending in a daggerlike foot, dangled casually over the outcropping, the spines rasping across the rock. Siona gasped as that one leg was joined by another. She gasped louder when the pair of legs was joined by a set of serrated fangs, above which rested four sets of glaring black eyes. And she screamed when the creature sprang down to a ledge right above the hare, landing on all eight of its jointed legs.

"Thank you for that lovely and inspiring introduction. I am ready for my lunch now," said the spider, sharpening a fang against a sharp spine. "Who wants to be eaten first?"

5

Escape through the Black Lava Tube

THE SPIDER SPUTTERED BEHIND THE thick veil of purple ink. He pounded the tide pool floor with his eight legs. A cloud of silt rose around the spider to meet the lingering purple veil. The spider coughed. He kicked an empty shell and laughed when it broke.

"I'm not through with you yet," the spider screeched in the direction of his departed lunch. The spider turned on his long legs and headed to a tower of rock in the middle of the tide pool. At the base of the tower, the purple spider parted the red algae before a wide black crack in the rock with his powerful front legs. "Uncle Rupert," he called, "would you like to join me for lunch?" Out of the blackness of the rock, came an even blacker, bigger, and more fearsome sea spider.

"That ink of yours is one special trick," gasped Reilly.

The three animals were breathing hard, grateful for the sanctuary of distance between them and the spider. They had escaped to the far side of the pool where the thundering surf drowned the screams of the spider they had left behind.

"Do you think so? Do you like my trick?" asked Harold the Sea Hare. "It's a trick that has been in my family for generations. I don't know how it all started, but it does seem rather effective. It is a bit surprising that I am the only one of the three of us that can do this trick."

"Well, we all have our limitations," said Reilly, looking at Siona.

Siona could not help but think that they all had their special talents as well. She had her mighty tail, the ragworm his fangs, and the hare his tricky purple ink and special rhinophores.

"Yes, that's certainly true. We all have our limitations." The sea hare sighed, his rhinophores drooping.

Siona flicked her tail and approached the hare. "I am on a mission, you know, to find Clarissa the Clairvoyant Clam and her friend the lovely Spanish dancer. Maybe they could help you find out more about your ink"—Siona paused—"and why you are so special."

"Yes, thank you. I would like to know how I came to be so special. I have never really thought about it before. But it must be true. I am special," the hare said, swishing his rhinophores in a circle. "I'd also like to know why red algae are so tasty. In fact, there is one patch of red algae that is so divine that every time I go there for a nibble, it's like being there for the first time, even though I have a really great memory. I can be in the exact same spot, day after day, a little to the left of the big white rock with pebbles in its cracks, and it's as if I have never been there before. The red algae are that delicious! How can that be? I just don't understand it."

As the hare spoke, the earth spun, rotating around the sun. With the universe expanding, the entire solar system—the sun, the earth, and all the other planets and their moons—sped at 43,000 miles per hour through space. And with that, cosmically speaking, the sea hare was indeed never in the same spot twice, even when eating the red algae a little to the left of the big white rock with pebbles in its cracks.

"Well," said Reilly, "we need to find Sydney the Sea Star. He has the fastest tube feet of any star, and he knows the secret passageway to the tide pool where Clarissa and the Spanish dancer live." And the worm called out to Sydney the Sea Star, letting the water convey the summons. "Now we will have to wait," he said to Siona.

Siona cringed at those words. "I'm not so good at that waiting stuff," she said, her tail drooping.

"How about giving me some more coaching while we wait?" Reilly suggested. "I could use some help on that impossible upside-down, inside-out circle."

Before Siona could reply, the worm gathered speed, diving down and then soaring straight up, his paddles thrashing. Up, up, up he went. Reaching the apex of his journey, he arched his back, making ready for his mad descent. His fangs opened wide and horrible. Down he went, his fangs snapping shut with a bang. Caught in the turbulence of his own trajectory, he spiraled out of control, narrowly missing a sharp rock and hitting the sandy bottom with a belly flop, creating a tiny crater. The worm shook himself, forcing a grin.

"Are you all right?" asked Harold, his rhinophores twitching.

"Would you mind doing that again?" Siona asked the worm.

"What? Are you crazy?" cried the hare. "He nearly got himself killed!"

The neurons, or brain cells, in Siona's big head were running complex computations, calculating shear forces and other factors. "Try moving your paddles together during the climb up, and when you reach the top of the circle and are heading back down, hold the first three pairs of paddles right next to your body. Hold them as flat as you can, but keep paddling with all the other paddles. Can you do that?"

"I think so," said the worm, shaking sand from his segments. He repeated the maneuver, synchronizing his paddles. Up he went, and reaching the apex of the circle, his fangs opened wide. Down he plunged, holding three pairs of paddles tight against his body. Siona and the hare watched, holding their breath. The fourth and fifth pair of paddles caught the turbulence. The worm shuddered. Vibrating, he tumbled to the left. Lifting his paddles on the left, he corrected his course and skidded across the sand. It was not a perfect circle, but it was pretty close. A big grin covered the worm's fierce face.

"Thank you, Siona! That was my best inside-out, upside-down circle!" The worm rolled onto his back in joy, clapping with his paddles.

"Great job!" said Siona. "Maybe you can try one more."

"There he is!" called Reilly, pointing with a fang to a rock, over which clambered an orange sea star.

"Did I hear someone call my name?" asked the star.

Siona looked up at the rock. The star moved in fits and starts, limping across the rock. How could this star be the fastest star ever? All her hopes were on this sole star, but something was missing. Siona blinked her eyes. The star had only four arms! Where the fifth arm should have been was a bumpy stump. Siona heard Reilly gasp too. "What happened to your fifth arm? Where did it go?" she asked.

Sydney the Sea Star sighed. His tube feet in the two left arms extended, while the tube feet in the two right arms shrunk. This was followed by the reverse. The right side would rise and left side would drop, turning the star into a seesaw as he teetered at the edge of the rock. "I used to be the fastest star in all the known tide pools." The star sighed again. "Now my hydraulic systems are a mess! I'll never be same star again."

With only four arms, Sydney's hydraulic systems were in shambles. His plumbing had to be precisely regulated through pipes, valves, and whatnot to draw in seawater. That is how the star moved—by moving seawater into and out of his three hundred tube feet, minus those gone missing with the fifth arm. Seawater should flow through the pipes (canals) into little bags (ampullae) above each tube foot. Water from those little bags was supposed to squirt into a tube foot to make it extend. But now the flow of water in Sydney's hydraulic systems seemed to be beyond his control. He had been forced to compensate. The suction he could generate from each foot had increased over twofold, and from each little foot he secreted temporary glue-like widgets to keep from sliding off the rocks. When he walked now, he left a little trail of sea star footprints—polka dots on the rocks. But even these adaptations were not enough to compensate for damage to his hydraulics.

"What happened?" asked Siona and Reilly together.

"I took a direct hit"—the star tried to make his way across the rock—"at close range from the supersonic bubbles of a pistol shrimp. Blasted my arm right off." He cried, and two arms lifted up from the rock. He lost his hold, fell from the rocks, and landed upside down on the tide pool floor in a puff of sand and debris.

Siona could see the stump of the fifth arm. Tube feet moved in all directions. It took the star some time to right himself.

"Even destroyed the stem cells that I need to grow a new arm." When the star was right side up, he sighed again. "Two big squirt larvae, though not quite as large as you, tried to fix my arm with their nanoscale whiskers and cellulose blend, but I don't know if my arm will ever grow back."

"I think you are a brave star," said Siona. "A sea squirt used that same stuff to fix my tail after it got burned by green slime on some red rocks and by the innards of a sponge. See? Look." She showed her tail to the star.

Sydney's tube feet stopped moving. He was perfectly still. "You survived the green slime and the inside of a sponge?"

Siona nodded.

"You must be special," said the star, continuing to sigh. "And I'm a broken misfit now."

"But I'm a misfit too," said Siona. "Look at me. My head is too big, and my tail is too long."

The star looked at her askance. "Are you really a sea squirt larva? I've never seen one like you before."

"She's special is all," said Harold the Sea Hare, pointing a rhinophore at the star. "She just has an oversized tail and wants to do some good with what she's got."

"Hmm," said the star, "maybe I could do some good with what I've still got too."

"We can be misfits together!" said Siona.

The star looked at Siona and slapped his four good arms down on the sand. "Tell me," he said, "what can I do for you?" This time he did not sigh.

And Siona told Sydney of her mission to find Clarissa the Clairvoyant Clam and the lovely Spanish dancer, so that she could keep her tail and keep on swimming. She pointed to Harold, noting that they all wanted to know why he was so special. Harold smiled, his rhinophores sweeping in wide circles. She described the fierce acrobatic beauty of Reilly's inside-out, upside-down circle and that they were all desperate to see that circle completed. Reilly shook his head, but he smiled with his fangs arching perfectly.

The star nodded, pointing in the direction of a secret passageway with one of his four good arms. "I can take you to the passage now," said Sydney, "but we will have to wait for the tide. The water level is too low now."

Siona flicked her tail; she did not like the idea of waiting even for a moment. Time, she knew, was against her. And waiting for the tide to show up did not seem at all necessary. *Who is that anyway?* she thought.

Sydney led them in fits and starts, closer to the sound of the pounding ocean, where the waves broke against the rocks just beyond the protective walls of the tide pool. "See—look there," said the star, raising one of his four arms and waving a few tube feet in a somewhat coordinated effort to point.

There, formed millions of years ago by scorching lava, followed by centuries of flowing water, a narrow tunnel had cut its way through the rock, ending near the top of the tide pool. Light spilled an inch or two into the opening of the tube. A tumble of rocks provided an uneven stairway up to the passage.

"That's it," he said triumphantly. "That's the lava tube that connects this tide pool to the next!"

Reilly paddled up the rocks and looked with skepticism into the darkness of the tunnel. He scraped his fangs against the walls of the tunnel, as if to test their strength. Harold peered over Reilly's left fang with trepidation, his rhinophores shaking. Siona swam to the opening, crossing over the threshold into darkness.

"Let's go," she said. "The tide can join us later."

Sydney laughed, and losing control of most of his feet, he nearly tumbled off the rock staircase. The star used his arms (as best he could) to show Siona the meaning of the tide—that the water in the pool rose and fell, pulled by the moon and pushed by a spinning planet. The tide had to be high for their safe travel through the passage; the lava tube had to be completely filled with water. The star explained that at the halfway point, the ceiling of the tube had collapsed. What had been the ceiling was a pile of rubble on the lava tube floor. If the water in the tube was too low, they would not be able to swim over the rubble. They would be stuck, peering through a hole in the rock ceiling at the clouds above.

Siona sighed. "So I guess we just have to wait."

"Yes, absolutely. We will have to wait," repeated Harold. "Hmm, those particular red algae over there look especially tasty," said the hare with his rhinophores perking up. Waddling to the clump of algae, the hare sang out, "Oh yummy, yummy in my tummy! There is nothing better in the whole universe than sweet, sweet algae."

"What if I start changing here? What if I run out of time?" whispered Siona, her voice hardly audible above the happy humming of the hare.

Harold stopped midway between the algae and his companions. He turned to look back at Siona. But his rhinophores caught the indescribable scent of the algae, capturing his attention. He watched them sway in the gentle currents. He took a deep breath and turned his gaze back to Siona. "I have a song for you, Siona," he called, coughing to clear his throat. "It's called 'Ode to Siona the Sea Squirt.'"

His left rhinophore extended toward the young squirt, while the right rhinophore continued to stretch toward the red algae. Harold seemed a bit unbalanced; one rhinophore pushed him back, and the other pulled him forward. His left rhinophore twitched toward Siona, and slowly, the right appendage swung away from the intoxicating red algae until both rhinophores were finally in agreement, focused on the young squirt. Harold regained his balance.

And he began to sing. From his squishy and soft body, his song emerged with operatic vibrato. Reilly and Sydney halted their conversation. Rotifers near and far stayed as little balls. Adult sea squirts stopped squirting; sea squirt larvae paused in their search for a perfect rock. The sea stars sucked in their tube feet, and a great many of them slid off rock walls. Snails emerged from their shells; clams and proto-scallops opened theirs. But the sea spiders laughed at their luck. Attracted by the song, they marched, sharpening their serrated fangs as they approached. With anticipation, the spiders headed to the dinner theater.

The sea hare sang the song, "Ode to Siona the Sea Squirt."

It's you that I shall ever adore
With each and every rhinophore.
You smell so sweet,
It's such a treat
That not even the biggest and bestest algae can beat.

'Cause she loves to swim in the open pools.
Her dreams are like the brightest jewels,

To become what she wills and not
What she ought.
For it is the rock that she has left unsought,
Determined to change what is wrought.

Of her chances who can say
That she'll find a way to change today.

What of that misfit misunderstood,
Believing her tail can bring some good.
A hope, a chance, to follow her call,
And lend understanding to one and all.

It's you that I shall ever adore
With each and every rhinophore.
You smell so sweet,
It is such a treat!
Your being will forever more
Go down in the history of animal lore.

The song ended, rolling with its own rhythm in the waves, leaving Harold breathing hard, his rhinophores twitching and taut. As the song subsided, the cheers of the tide pool creatures rose in a wave of applause. Harold smiled a wee, shy smile. Reilly knocked his paddles and his fangs together in syncopation. Sydney's tube feet abruptly extended, pushing him up so high that he hovered and spun above the sandy bottom of the tide pool like a four-pointed star in the heavens.

And Siona cried. "I am a misfit, but you made me feel like I might be special." She sobbed into her tail. Harold glided to her side. He touched her delicate body with his rhinophores. Reilly and Sydney made their way to Siona and Harold. They gathered together—the four unlikely creatures, all creatures of creation, sharing a moment long ago in time.

Siona lifted her head from her tail and caught the sea hare's gaze. A slow, beatific smile replaced her tears. She touched the hare with her tail. The rhinophores of the sea hare swayed in response. And he, too, felt special indeed.

As the song ended there was a disturbance above the red algae. Sydney took some time to regain control of a couple of dozen tube feet and managed to attach to the large rock where Reilly and Siona had taken positions during the musical performance. It was then that the animals took note of the tiny avalanche of grains of sand and small pebbles that cascaded down from the rocks above the red algae. One good-sized pebble crushed a number of red algae, and a single bubble escaped. In unison, the animals turned their gazes to the bubble and followed its ascent. Up, up it went until it reached a dark, cavernous wound on the rock face. From this cut in the rock emerged a monstrous black sea spider. It unfolded its mighty front legs, ready to lunge. The four creatures below cried out, and a plume of dark purple ink erupted from the sea hare's backside. The worm, squirt, star, and hare fled in the opposite direction, away from the black spider. But they did not get very far. Before them stood the purple sea spider, with four of its spiked legs piercing the water like bayonets.

"This way!" screamed Sydney. "Into the lava tube! Hurry! Hurry! Go! Go! Reilly, take Siona in your fangs; just go! Harold, follow me and spray that juice of yours again!"

Reilly grabbed Siona, holding her a bit too tight. She cried out, but Reilly paid no attention. His paddles raked the floor of the lava tube as he escaped into the darkness. Right behind him fled Sydney, his tube feet pumping.

"Squirt your ink! Squirt your ink!" screamed Sydney to the sea hare. Sydney glanced back over one of his arms. Harold was lumbering just ahead of the purple spider.

"I can't squirt anymore. I can't. I used up all my ink! Help! Help!" cried Harold.

Siona wiggled in the jaws of the ragworm. "Reilly, we have to help him. He saved us; now he needs our help."

"He needs *my* help, and this is *not* the time to disagree. Go on, Siona. Get to the next tide pool. We will be right behind you. Now go!" He released Siona from his tight grip. "*Go! Go now, Siona!*" cried Reilly. He spun around and headed back down through the darkness toward two sets of fangs much larger than his own.

Siona swam away from the screeching spiders for a few strokes. She heard Harold cry out. "The spiders are gaining on me! I'm out of juice. My apologies! Help! Help!"

She stopped and turned around, staring down the dark tunnel. By her estimation, Harold was only about twenty centimeters ahead of the spiders. And the spiders were racing at a speed ten times that of the hare. Siona calculated how much time it would take before the spiders would catch the hare. She gasped. By her calculation, Harold had only two minutes and twelve seconds. She had to do something to slow down the spiders.

The spiders screeched again, their harsh voices echoing in the gloom. Siona, with a beat of her tail, headed back to the hare and spiders. Ahead of her, Reilly was a dark shadow as he, too, sped back to the star and the hare. Sydney was well ahead of the hare, his tube feet pumping at what seemed like warp speed for a star with only four arms. He looked back over one arm.

"Come on, Harold!" cried the star. "You can do it! Slither as fast as you can go!" Sydney, still looking backward, slammed one of his four arms down against the rock. The arm caught, wedged in a crack. If he'd had all five of his arms and better control of his hydraulics, he might have been able to get out of the crack. Instead, Sydney's three other arms sailed up into the narrow tube, striking Reilly, who had just reached the star. The worm was knocked down to the floor of the tube. In a jumble of paddles and arms, the two creatures panted on the floor of the lava tube. In the commotion, neither Reilly nor Sydney saw Siona swim past. Sixty seconds later, Reilly had figured out how to free the star's arm. Reilly squeezed himself against the side of the tube so that the star could pass. Reilly called to Harold to encourage the flight of the hare from the spiders.

Barely above the screeching of the spiders, they heard Siona cry out. "You guys keep going! I'm going to stop the spiders."

"Siona, no! Get back here right now. *Stop!*" cried Reilly. In frustration he knocked a paddle to his head, and then bolted down the lava tube to the spiders, to Siona, to save a young life that surely would be lost.

"Those darn spiders aren't going to hurt my friends. I'm going to slow them down so you can get away!" yelled Siona, ignoring the cries of the worm. She swam past Harold, urging him on.

Siona swam right up to the purple spider. He was much bigger than she had remembered. His great serrated fangs opened—the image of brutality. His eight eyes glowed in the dim light. He advanced on the tiny larva, scraping the sides of the lava tube with his sharp spines.

"Oh! Our snack has arrived," sneered the purple spider through his serrated fangs.

"I'm not your snack! You stop right where you are!" Siona said boldly, but she trembled, and tears filled her eyes as she stared up at the spider towering above.

"Don't worry, little squirt. You won't feel a thing. It all will be over before you know it. And you will be part of me. And we will be one. And I certainly will take pleasure in that!"

Siona lashed out with her mighty tail. The spider screamed. Seven eyes now gleamed in the darkness. The spider lunged forward with a long front leg, pinning Siona down to the rock below.

The black spider arrived, snarling right behind his purple relative.

"Good catch," said the black spider.

"Yes, yes," said the purple spider. He turned his attention to Siona. "And remember how I said that you would not feel a thing?" He pressed his sharp, pointy leg against her body. "Well, you can forget that now." Siona struggled against the sharp weight of the leg. The purple spider laughed. "She's fighting me, as if she thinks she can get away," said the purple spider, bending low, his fangs brushing across her body. "This one smells so sweet and fresh."

"I do like my larvae fresh," said the black spider.

"Oh, yes, I like mine right out of the egg. Once they start to grow up and show those nasty nanoscale whiskers, they get such a bitter aftertaste, but a young one like this is so sweet and tasty. It's a pity that this one will not be growing up, but we have to live too." The purple spider looked at the black spider. "Uncle Rupert, would you like to take the first bite?"

"I'll take the first bite," said Reilly, appearing out of the darkness. The fangs of the worm snapped shut above the pointed foot of the purple spider. Nothing happened.

The spider laughed. Reilly, still holding on, looked up at the serrated fangs above and the seven eyes glaring down. Reilly tried to squeeze his fangs tighter. Nothing. The Spider pushed his pointed foot harder against Siona. She struggled, fighting. She whipped her tail, striking the fangs of the worm, knocking them up along the pointed foot of the spider to the joint that connected the foot to the rest of the spider's leg. There, the exoskeleton of the spider was at its weakest. It was there that Reilly snapped his fangs shut with such acceleration that Siona could not see how fast they moved. She heard the sharp crack, followed by a howl. The weight that pinned her down vanished. She was free.

Reilly, his voice harsh, cried, "Swim, swim!" Siona bolted away from the screaming spiders. The right front leg of the purple spider was significantly shorter than the others. The purple spider leaped back in anger and pain, his legs moving in all directions. The two spiders became a tangled mass of jaws, body parts, and sixteen snarled legs. Reilly turned, following Siona. Ahead, a pale patch of light grew brighter. The light made silhouettes of the hare and star.

"This is just what I was worried about," lamented Sydney. "We didn't have time to wait until the tide came in. The water level is too low. We won't be able to cross!"

Blocking their escape was an impenetrable mound of hard black lava. Above the black mound, the sky was bright and blue. Occasionally a wave came close to splashing in from above, but there was no strength in the waves now. The animals saw the spray from the waves, but that was all. Above the mound was nothing but inhospitable air. These sea-dwelling creatures could not survive out of water beyond a few short moments. It would take more than two hundred million years of change, alteration, and trial and error before the first animals could eke out a living on land. And this migration from water to land, this terrestrialization, would become one of the most significant transitions in the history of life. But none of them—not the hare, the worm, the star, or the squirt—had the necessary bits of biology to live long out of water.

From the darkness, the spiders shrieked as they untangled their eight pairs of legs.

"Not only am I ravenous, but now I am furious," the purple spider screamed at Siona. "Tell that mutant ragworm friend of yours that I am going to pull off each one of his paddles and eat them one by one, and I'll make you watch until I eat you too!"

The water in the tube grew turbulent, vibrating, shaking the four desperate animals. The spiders were approaching fast, scraping their rough bodies and sharp spines against the lava tube wall like fingernails on a blackboard. Had Siona, Reilly, Harold, and Sydney had hair, it would have stood straight up. But hair and fur would be an adaptation that would have to wait for the arrival of mammals, hundreds of millions years after this story takes place.

"Siona, this time you have to go. Keep going. We will be right behind you," said Reilly, staring down the tunnel toward the screeching spiders.

Siona started to protest. "I'm not going to le—"

Reilly grabbed her in his fangs before she could finish, rose up on the tip of his tail, arched his back, and then whipped his entire body forward, releasing the squirt like a pitcher on a baseball mound throwing a fastball. Siona first hit a pool of shallow water, bounced, and landed, gasping, on a rock ledge.

"Help me! Help me!" she cried.

Reilly rose up on all his paddles and scrambled over the rock ruins. He reached Siona and lifted her gently from the rough rock and inhospitable air and dropped her down into the soothing water on the other side of the rubble. Had Reilly had lungs they would have been burning, but Reilly did not even have gills. Like the annelid he was, he breathed through his epidermis, or skin, so his whole body was inflamed.

No sooner had she been saved than Siona heard Harold wail, "Help me! *Help me!*" She saw Reilly rise up on his stiff tail paddles to peer above the rubble. On the other side of the rubble, she could hear the spiders closing in. She closed her eyes in despair. What could be done now? She felt helpless in her pool at the base of the rubble. She looked up at the worm. She saw him hang his head, his paddles drooping, as he slid back down into a small shallow pool of water cupped in the rubble of the rock.

"It's okay," said a calm voice behind her. Siona gasped. A bright, white clam rose from the watery depths like a submarine ready to support the besieged battleships of her allies. Her shell opened, and the sunlight falling through the gash in the lava tube played on the iridescent mother of pearl in opaline hues of yellow, pink, green, and blue.

"Pleased to meet you, Siona," said the clam. "You can call me Clarissa."

Siona stared at the clam, her eyes wide.

"Reilly!" cried Siona. "Reilly, there is someone here to help us!" Siona took a deep breath. She had finally found Clarissa the Clairvoyant Clam, the clam of her destiny. With the ongoing siege, it did not occur to Siona that perhaps the clam had actually found her. Reilly glanced down, and seeing the clam, his paddles rose, and he clicked his fangs.

"Now is not the time for introductions. Reilly, take a deep breath. Get ready to go to the top on the rocks," said the clam calmly. "I will follow you. Use your fangs to save your friends."

Reilly called over the ruins, "Sydney, use three of your arms and hold on to Harold with all your might. Bend your fourth arm back toward me. Do it now!"

"Hold your breath in your gills, both of you!" cried Siona to the hare and star.

"But my tube feet are out of control. They aren't doing what I want at all!" cried the star in near hysterics. "My hydraulic systems are shot. I'm no good with only four arms!"

"Sydney," called the calm clam, "you can do this. You can control all 240 of your tube feet. You are the master of your feet!"

And with that encouragement, the star latched on to the squishy body of the sea hare with three of his strong arms. The fourth arm he bent toward Reilly. And both Sydney and Harold held their breath deep in their gills, which in this story is very possible.

"Now, Reilly, you know what to do," said the clam. "Climb to the top of the rubble and grab Sydney's arm in your fangs. I will be your anchor."

Reilly held his breath and raced to the top of the rubble. Right behind him came the clam. She opened her bivalve shell slightly, and Reilly wedged his tail between the two sides of the shell. Clarissa clamped the two halves of her shell together with vigor. Reilly winced.

Anchored by the clam, the worm flung himself forward, his fangs opened as wide as they could go without doing an inside-out, upside-down circle. He aimed with precision at the waving orange arm of the star and caught it in his fangs. As the worm lifted the star, the star's tube feet stretched precariously with the weight of the hare. But this time the majority of the feet obeyed their master, and 180 of them performed with precision, forming miniture suction cups, holding firm to the squishy body of the hare.

Reilly flung backward, arching his back; he was held in place by the weight of the clam. At the apex of his journey backward, he released his grip, casting the star and hare over the rocks. Through the hostile air the two beleaguered animals flew, a flashing of orange, tube feet moving every which way, rhinophores swishing, and all with wild calls of "Oh my! Whoa! Yikes! Eek!" But that was nothing compared to the screeching of the sea spiders. Deprived of another meal, the spiders were furious. They scrambled up the rocks after their prey. But in their anger and haste, they tripped over each other, falling back down to the bottom of the pile of rubble in yet another tangled mass. The sixteen legs between them was a liability. And despite the chaos of the flight over the rock ruins, the star and hare ended right-side up. Sydney's feet were pumping, and Harold slithered as fast as he could, his body swaying from side to side, while Siona swam ahead. Siona called to the worm and the clam, but they needed no encouragement to chase after their comrades into the darkness of the far side of the lava tube.

Siona could not hear the ocean roar over the screeching of the spiders. Pulled by the moon, high tide was well on its way. Pushed by the wind, a single great wave rose high on the shoulders of the incoming tide. No one saw the mighty wave from the bowels of the lava tube. It rose like a frothing and foaming sea serpent, colliding with the land, hurtling watery tentacles through the rip in the rock. On either side of the ruins, the great wave licked the rocks, chasing the fleeing prey to the exit and the pursuing predators back to the entrance. Siona did not see the spiders hurtling away, caught in the watery jaws of the turbulent wave, their legs twisting out of control. She could only imagine how they might end up, but it was far worse than she could ever guess. The spiders were flung together back into the tube until they ended up as a tight knot of tangled torsos and legs. It would take the two spiders two days before they could untangle their legs and free themselves of each other's company. And that would be the end of their mutual hunting escapades. To this day, the black and the purple spiders are never seen together, except when fighting turf wars over the tide pool.

As for the prey, the great wave ushered them from the narrows of the dark tube to the wide-open basin of the new tide pool with great haste. They spilled from the tube. Siona tumbled from the tube, falling to the left. Sydney fell to the tide pool floor upside down, his tube feet expanding and contracting as if still trying to flee. Harold followed, landing right on top of Sydney, only to be catapulted back up as the star's tube feet suddenly expanded. Sydney watched the hare somersault through the water.

"I'm sorry, Harold!" called the star.

"Oh no, Sydney; it is I who should apologize!" exclaimed the hare in mid-somersault. "I am sorry that I landed right on top of you!"

Shooting from the tube, Reilly banked hard to the right to avoid colliding with Harold and Sydney. He landed hard on the tide pool floor. The last to arrive was Clarissa the Clairvoyant Clam. She drifted with ease to the tide pool floor, welcoming the newcomers as she descended to the sand below.

The exit from the lava tube brought Siona and her companions into an enormous tide pool with a wide sandy basin, numerous tributaries, and luscious clumps of algae. They had reached a new world, rich in natural resources—sunlight, phosphate rocks, and bubbling sulfur. The sulfur reeked, but it was money, its elemental currency used to fund energy manufacturing and the production of biofuel. The sulfur fed the microbial mats. The mats pumped more nutrients into the pool. The phosphate rocks leached elemental phosphorous, feeding the algae, creating a dense pasture, and driving the diversity of the pool. With the abundance of life, there was also an abundance of dead things swirling in the water, their parts recycled, adding to the wealth of the new pool.

The creatures in this new pool did not look quite the same. The basic ideas were there, but the differences were in the details. The feathers of green-lipped proto-barnacles in this tide pool were yellow and white. The stars here were purple, not orange. There even were stars without arms, their bodies perfect pentagons. There were sea hares with solid spots but no circles. There were globular sponges, long lacy sponges, corals like trees and shrubs and tiny flower pots, and brachiopods on pedestals, their fan-shaped shells opened in hopeful grins. Schools of gilled lobopods sailed overhead, followed by scores of creatures just like Propikaia, except these boasted bright orange racing stripes. Anchored to black rocks, bright-white sea squirts swayed as one. At the periphery, a cluster of sea squirts grew—outcasts—their tunics tainted with orange stripes and blotches like unwanted birthmarks.

Built by ambitious engineers, there were highways of tunnels, tubes, and burrows. A priapulid worm labored to make a burrow bigger. Diurnal cousins of Helamite the Hallucigenia ambled on their fourteen-clawed legs across the tide pool basin, grazing on lush purple algae. Their long red and yellow spikes swayed as they moved. Bacrites, the precursors of squids and cuttlefish, with their long, straight shells, floated gracefully just below the surface of the water, their tentacles dangling. Covered with corrugated carbonaceous scales and spines, a family of *Wiwaxia corrugata* slithered through the algae. An *Opabina reglis* fluttered above, her paddles like feathers. She explored the tide pool floor with her long trunk-like proboscis; her five stalked eyes were on the lookout for danger. A lone *Odontogriphus omalus* crept in between the rocks among scores and scores of other animals with long Latin names, now long extinct.

There was a brilliant flash of red as a young ragworm paddled along the rocks of the new tide pool. Reilly blinked. His eyes opened wide, and his paddles fluttered. The bright red worm moved to take refuge in a clump of green algae. Siona glanced at the red ragworm, and she saw the creature gazing at Reilly, staring at his fangs. The paddles of the red ragworm fluttered like Reilly's. And Siona knew exactly what she had to do.

"Oh, Reilly!" Siona called in a high voice. "You saved us! You saved us all!" She, the hare, and the star gathered around the worm, patting his paddles and well-cut segments. "Reilly, you are my hero!" the animals called out with glee.

With the commotion, the young red ragworm slipped from behind the algae. As she did so, her eyes caught those of Reilly. Their eyes met. Reilly blinked and looked away. The red ragworm clicked her fangs and paddled behind the curtain of green algae again. As the red ragworm departed, Siona was sure that she heard Reilly's blood pumping faster through his five primordial peristaltic hearts.

Siona glanced at Clarissa, and the clam smiled. To see a clam smile was something special. Clarissa opened her shell just a bit, and the mother of pearl glistened and sparkled with iridescent light, a miniature sunrise of pastel colors.

Reilly swam toward the clam and encircled her with his paddles, hugging her tightly. Harold slithered along the sand and rested his rhinophores, one by one, on the smooth shell of the clam. Sydney tubed his way over. He likely did not want the clam to think that he thought she would be his next meal, so he reached out with a single arm, and to his astonishment, he touched her shell with a single tube foot, such was his newfound control over his hydraulics. Siona touched the clam with her tiny head. In this way, the creatures, from the largest to the smallest, gave their thanks.

Clarissa knew. They all knew. They all had been given another chance.

What would you do if you and your friends were given another chance—if you were able to escape predatory sea spiders and the perils of air without a good set of lungs? What if every day, when the sun rose and shone brilliantly, dancing through the trees, which arrived some 360 to 385 millions of years ago, or on wee blades of grass, which arose so much later, arriving only eighty million years ago and discovered in dinosaur coprolite (that is, fossilized dinosaur poop), you were given another chance? Isn't that what happens every new day? You get another chance?

* * *

Siona the human jumped from her grandfather's big rocking chair.

"That's what happened, minus the part about the dinosaur crapolite!" Siona hugged her mother. "You remembered that! That was ages ago. I was only eight years old when it happened."

"Yes, of course I remember," said Siona's mother. "I was thinking about that when Siona the Sea Squirt wanted to stop the spiders."

"I was so worried, like Siona when she saw her friends in trouble," Siona said. "That car was so big and going so fast. And that poor snake was right there. I had to help it; I had to."

"You took a big risk, but you gave that snake another chance." Siona's mother looked out the window. She bit her lip. Beneath the lowest branch of the tulip tree, a caterpillar twisted in midair, suspended on its silken thread. "You got another chance too," she said, swallowing. "And I'm so glad." She raised her hands to her eyes. Siona took her seat beside her mother and closed her eyes.

That day Siona could barely sit still. Her best friend, Gracie Alice, would be at her front door at any moment. Siona paced the floor. "I need something to do while I wait for Gracie Alice. I can't wait to see her again! She's been gone for two weeks, visiting her grandparents, and now she is back!" Siona sat down on the rocking chair and blew her nose into the hanky that her mother had stuffed into her pocket, glad that her cold was coming to an end. She pushed the hanky back into her pocket and rubbed her hands together. "I know," said Siona, bounding from the rocking chair. "I'll count the blades of grass in the backyard. And if Gracie Alice is still not here by the time I finish, then I'll count the leaves on the tulip tree in the front yard. That should keep me busy!" She raced out the kitchen door to the backyard. Siona knelt on the patio and began counting the blades of grass.

"Maybe you can count the blades in one square inch and then calculate the total number of blades in the backyard, based on the estimated square footage," suggested her mother, staring at her computer screen as she typed from the kitchen table.

"Fifty-two," called Siona from the backyard, with a blade of grass between her fingers. "I counted fifty-two blades of grass in about an inch of space." Siona stood, sizing up the lawn. "I never noticed how much the sun sparkles on the grass. I'll bet the sun sparkles on the leaves of the tulip tree too." Siona raced back into the house, running from the kitchen into the living room. She stopped at the large picture window. The leaves danced, glistening in the sun.

There was a knock on the door. Siona ran to the front door, swinging it wide open. There was Gracie Alice. Her hair glistened in the sunlight, as if a trillion tiny stars twinkled among the strands. The two girls hugged, laughing.

Siona clapped her hands together. "Did your grandmother show you another magic trick?" she asked, barely able to breathe out the words.

Gracie Alice nodded, and with a deft movement, she pulled a quarter from behind Siona's left ear.

"Do it again! Do it again!" cried Siona.

Gracie Alice reached forward and pulled out a quarter from Siona's right ear.

Siona squealed with delight. "You'll have to show me how to do that. My mom never has any quarters!" She held Gracie Alice's hand and led her down the front steps. "We'll be back by three!" Siona called to her mother.

"Sounds great," replied her mother, still typing on her computer from the kitchen.

The two girls set off, skipping down the sidewalk, their hands swinging between them, as they headed to their favorite place in the woods—a fortress of rocks hidden by blackberry bushes and a stand of young redwoods. Gracie Alice chatted about her adventures with her grandmother, and Siona laughed.

Siona came to a screeching stop and pointed down to a trail of ants and their loot, the carcass of a grasshopper. The two girls knelt on the sidewalk. En route to the grasshopper the ants clambered up and over a twig. Siona knelt down on the sidewalk and moved the twig from the path of the ants. The two-way traffic of the ant highway came to a halt. Some of the ant sisters reversed their course, some bumped into others. One ant that remained on top of the twig went down one side of the twig only to retract its steps, climbing up and over, up and over again.

"That doesn't seem like a very nice thing to do," said Gracie Alice.

"We're doing an experiment," said Siona, looking up from the ants. "Just watch the ants. They'll figure it out. They'll use their ol' factory systems and smell which way to go." Siona peered down at the ants. "That's what my dad says, and he studies bugs all day long."

Gracie Alice bent closer to the ants. "You and your dad sure know a lot."

It took one ant to bridge the expanse where the twig had been. The ant zigzagged across the chasm. Others followed, and the traffic on the ant highway resumed.

Siona looked up at Gracie Alice. "See?" she said. "They figured it out, all because of their ol' factory systems." Siona sniffled. She reached into her pocket, pulled out her hanky, and blew her nose. "My ol' factory systems aren't working so well today because my nose is all clogged up."

Across the street a ball went thump, thump, thump. Siona looked up from the ants. A group of children had gathered. Two boys bounced a ball between them. A third boy stared at Siona, and three girls waited for the commands of Marleen, the queen bee, who was a head taller than the others. Marleen stood with her arms akimbo.

"What are you doing over there?" asked Marleen.

"Watching some ants," Siona answered.

"Ants are stupid," said Marleen, flipping her hair back over her shoulders; it was a gold crown and cape waving in the sun.

"Ants can talk," said Siona in defense of the ants. "That's what my dad says, and he should know because he studies ants and bugs. He's an insectologist."

The boys stopped bouncing the ball. The thump-thump of the ball was replaced by the laughter of the queen and her subjects. Siona heard them laugh.

"Like father, like daughter."

"No wonder she is so weird."

"Who would study bugs? Gross!"

They did not even try to whisper. Their words crossed the street, and those words stung. Siona looked down. The ants marched.

"You are a weirdo," said Marleen. She tilted up her chin, a narrow smile pushing the corners of her mouth across her perfect face. "And my parents told me that your mother works with slime." Her subjects keeled over, holding their bellies, their laughter turning to shrieks. Bugs and slime!

Siona made a fist with her hand. "My mother collects slime samples so she can understand the whole world! She's a marine biologist!"

"Siona's mother is a slime collector!" cried one of the girls.

"A garbage collector!" cried another.

Siona jumped up, her face red. "My mother is not a garbage collector! What my mother does is really important!"

"Garbage collector, garbage collector!" the children screamed in a tight circle around Marleen. "Slime is more important than Siona."

Marleen, the queen, raised her hands. Her subjects quieted, their taunts quelled. Marlene brushed her fingers through her hair. She and Gracie Alice held the same colors in common. "Gracie Alice, come to my house," she commanded. She raised her eyebrows. "My mother made some fudgy brownies, and you can have one—you can have two—if you stop playing with that weirdo girl with slime-colored hair."

Siona opened her eyes wide. Her jaw dropped open. She cast an uneasy glance at Gracie Alice, her best friend, the harbor of her secrets, the one with whom she'd made her first batch of cookies. Together they'd picked yellow and white flowers from the forest floor, decorating their secret rock fortress in the shade of young redwoods.

"My hair is not slime-colored!" screamed Siona. And she sneezed. Snot exploded from her nose.

"Gross!" cried the children. The queen howled. A subject pointed at Siona, saying, "Look at all that slime."

The laughter cut the air. Siona wiped her nose on her sleeve, leaving a silver trail sparkling in the sun. Tears spilled down her cheeks. The boy who held the ball laughed so hard that it slipped from his hands, escaped to the sidewalk, and collided with a parked car. Under the car, a garter snake woke from its nap and, startled, slithered into the street. Siona saw the snake sliding, a yellow stripe on its back making waves. She did not see the green Honda that turned the corner, heading for the snake, until it was almost too late. In the corner of her eye, she saw it. Motion detected—danger in the mass of metal and dark green. The snake did not have a chance. Siona knew that there was only one thing to do. She had to make the car stop. Siona jumped into the street, placing her body between the oncoming car and the snake. Her arms waved above her head.

"*Stop! Stop!*" Siona screamed at the oncoming car. The car honked a long wail. The tires, shrieking in reply, left long black streaks. The laughter of the children turned to screams. Gracie Alice cried out. Siona bent down to pick up the snake and then ran, cradling the snake in her hands, into the queen's territory on the other side of the street.

"I'm sorry! I'm sorry," Siona called to the startled driver. She held up the snake above her head in explanation of her actions. The frightened snake musked a mix of urine and feces that slid through Siona's fingers, to her hair, and onto her cheek—a blotch of yellow and brown. It reeked.

The queen and her court of girls held their noses.

"Slimy, stinky Siona!" cried one of the boys. "Let's get that snake!"

Siona whirled on her heels and sprinted down Talisman Street, with the snake twisting and curling in her fingers, its stench in the air. The boys followed in pursuit.

"Let's kill that snake," cried the other boy.

Siona raced down the street, passing a surfer pulling his longboard from the top of his jeep; the sunlight a halo of gold in his curls. He pivoted, with the board perpendicular to street, a barricade before the boys. They skidded to stop.

"Whoa, dudes!" said the surfer, giving the boys a fatherly smile. With the toss of his chin, he pointed back down the street to Gracie Alice. "There's some real magic brewing there." The boys stared up at the surfer, took several steps backward, and turned around.

"I'll show you a magic trick," called Gracie Alice to the boys, who were on their way back.

"That snake stinks! Get over here!" cried the queen to the boys. "Come on. Let's get some brownies." She bent down, picked up a rock, and tossed it in the air. She caught it in the palm of her hand with long thin fingers. "You come too," the Queen said to Gracie Alice, "and show us your magic tricks, or that snake is history."

Siona turned back long enough to see Gracie Alice crossing the street to join the court of the queen. Abandoned by her best friend, she ran faster, gripping the snake. Tears, caught in the pull of the earth, cascaded down her cheeks. Her nose ran too. She turned right on Fifty-First Street, past the sign proclaiming Dead End. At the end of the road, she hit the path in the forest, her feet smashing twigs and pine needles. She pounded down the path in the light and shadow between the narrow trunks of trees. She reached the rock fortress—the boulders behind the blackberries, the two heads of giants tipped together forming an upside-down V, into which Siona and the snake escaped.

Siona panted, catching her breath, her shoulders heaving. "I'm sorry," she said to the snake, "for taking you so far from your home." She brushed her sleeve across her nose. Her hands reeked from the fear of the snake. Her hair reeked too. She bent down and opened her hands on the damp earth littered with the withered white and yellow flowers she and Gracie Alice had picked weeks ago. The snake streaked from her fingers, disappearing into the grass dappled with sunlight. Siona sat down in the upside-down V of the boulders and leaned against the cold rock. She pulled her knees to her chest, wrapping her arms around her shins. "Why am I such a weirdo?" she cried to her knees.

Later that afternoon, Siona's mother washed her daughter's face, hands, arms, and hair with tomato juice, followed by soap and shampoo. It was not until her mother had covered Siona's head with a towel and worked to dry her daughter's hair that Siona cried.

Beneath the towel, Siona wailed. "Why am I such a weirdo?"

Her mother knelt down on her knees, lifted up the towel, and let it drop over her head—mother and daughter together under the canopy of the towel. She placed her hands on Siona's shoulders. Siona cried again. Her nose ran. Her mother, lifting up the towel for a moment, retrieved a hanky from the bathroom counter. Siona blew her nose and explained to her mother why she was such a weirdo. Only a weirdo would stop to watch a bunch of stupid ants or try to save a snake. And if that wasn't bad enough, the school queen bee said her hair was the color of slime, and the other kids teased her that her own mother was a garbage collector!

"Siona," said her mother, "every species on this planet needs what others might call the weirdos and the outliers. Those are the special ones."

Later, after Siona's hair was dry, there was a knock on the door. It was Gracie Alice. "What do you want?" asked Siona with a sullen pout from the rocking chair. Gracie Alice sat down on the chair. Siona slid to the other side as far as she could and crossed her arms. Gracie Alice reached into her pocket, took out a napkin, and unwrapped it on her lap. Inside were two fudgy brownies. She handed one to Siona.

"Siona," said Gracie Alice, "I never took one bite of those brownies when I was at that girl's house." She smiled. "But I took these for us."

"Oh, Gracie Alice!" cried Siona, hugging her best friend. And Gracie Alice hugged Siona back, even though Siona still smelled slighty of snake.

"You saved that snake today," said Gracie Alice. "Nobody else would have done that."

"That's because I'm a weirdo," said Siona.

Gracie Alice laughed. "Me too." She gave Siona another hug and took a big bite from the brownie. She smiled, brown covering the white of her teeth.

Siona took a bite of her brownie and the two best friends sat munching the queen bee's fudgy brownies.

"Do you want to see if we can find some ants in the backyard?" asked Siona, finishing her brownie.

"I sure do!" said Gracie Alice.

Siona jumped up, leading the way. She opened the door to the backyard, and out they both sprang into the sunlight that glistened on the blades of grass and danced on the leaves of the trees.

Siona opened her eyes and leaned against her mother as they sat on the rocking chair. "We were lucky that day, both the snake and me. We both could have been hit by that car, but we both got another chance. I hope that Siona the Sea Squirt will be lucky too."

"Yes," said Siona's mother. "I wish I ..." She looked out the window. The caterpillar beneath the lowest branch of the tulip tree still lingered in midair, but now a feather was caught in the silken thread. The feather had had the entirety of all the sky in which to flutter and fall, yet it had struck a thread not much thicker than a human hair. The feather caught the breeze, and the caterpillar spun on its precarious connection to the tree. "That I had been there to save ..." Pushed by the breeze, the silken thread snapped. With no cupped hands to block its fall, the caterpillar fell to the ground, its chances over.

6

The Trilobite's Tale

A S THE FOUR UNLIKELY INVERTEBRATES celebrated their luck, the
sea beyond the protective walls of the tide pool grew restless.
Wave after wave crashed up against the rocks, as if the sea itself wished
to peer over the lip of stone. At the far side of the tide pool, an occasional
wave was successful, breaching the boundary of the rocks, churning the
sand, and then withdrawing out to the open sea.

For a long time, waves had collided with the land. The waves rolling
in from the sea wrote their stories on the rocky shore. A single wave on
the hard, sharp rock did not leave a trace except for sea foam and froth.
But slowly, over a long, long time, the sea shaped and molded even
the hardest stone. Caressed by the sea, new grooves were cut into the
rock. Sharp, pointed rock yielded with time in the company of waves,
gradually mellowing to a smooth surface.

Siona the Sea Squirt was the first to speak. "I have been searching
for you ever since I hatched from my egg—practically my entire life!"
she cried to the clam, telling Clarissa how she had been warned that
her journey would end in failure. But her hopes and dreams kept her
going against the odds. Siona told the clam how she had been helped
by the ragworm, the star, and the hare. And that had it not been for the
courage of her companions, she never would have made it so far. She
would likely have been digested by a sponge or eaten by a sea spider.

"I want to swim free. I don't want to grow up with my head stuck to a rock for the rest of my life. I think I can do a lot of good with my tail," said Siona.

Siona went on to tell Clarissa what she had learned of the world so far—that it contained different creatures with different talents. "There must be a way to change, or how could there be all of us—a worm, a star, and a hare. And yes, there are spiders and pistol shrimp too. And we are so different. There must be a way to change!"

Clarissa nodded as only a clam can. "Siona, you have many questions, and you and your companions have traveled far. But your journey is not quite over. You don't seek me but the trilobite, my cousin's cousin's cousin. You are very tired and weary. The Spanish dancer has arrived to assist you. She comes to us from the deep ocean and has seen many a sight."

Rising from the tide pool floor, the bright red-yellow-and-orange dancer approached like a magical flying carpet, her body rocking, twirling, and tipping. When she reached the others, she hovered above the sandy bottom of the pool. The animals nodded their acknowledgment of Dancer. She waved in silence at each of them. They had never seen a creature quite like her.

"She is very special," whispered Harold to Siona, and Siona nodded in agreement.

Clarissa moved to Dancer's back and motioned for the others to follow. It took some time getting used to the undulating movements of the dancer. Clarissa held gently to Dancer's gills with her bivalve shell. Reilly balanced on the undulating body. Siona rolled up in the soft gills and could have fallen fast asleep as easily as any exhausted child on a rocking chair. Sydney, who was desperately trying to hold on to both Dancer and Harold, by virtue of his feet, found, to his chagrin, that he again had very little control. Unfortunately, both Sydney and Harold fell off the back a number of times. Each time, Dancer waited patiently for the two invertebrates to regain their composure and clamber back on board. Sydney quietly cursed his bad luck about his wayward tube feet. And Harold pouted each time he hit the sand.

On the back of the Spanish dancer, the animals sailed through a curtain of algae and came to a stop. Clarissa indicated that they should dismount and gestured toward the massive rock wall before them. In the late-afternoon sun, long shadows stretched across the face of the rock.

From a dark gash in the rock, the trilobite emerged. He looked a little like a roly-poly pill bug but much bigger and wider. His antennae twitched. The trilobite shook the long spines that formed a horseshoe-like arc, starting from his head and ending in cascading sharp points about a third of the way down his body. A second set of long spines erupted from the left and right pleural lobes, curving gracefully from his body like a second horseshoe. A slow smile emerged across his midnight-black face. The trilobite nodded. So black was his armor that he seemed to be made of the same shadows that played on the rock wall. He was an exceptionally rare creature, his formation another of nature's pilot experiments. It would take another million years or so for his kind to catch on and proliferate.

Millions and millions of years ago, there were hundreds of thousands of these creatures. What of them today? Their stories are left in stone, housed under bright lights in glass cases in museums and galleries and on dusty fireplace mantels, reduced to fossilized imprints—brief excerpts from the play of life.

As the trilobite stepped forward onto a narrow ledge, he caught the sun. His shadow played across the rock, larger than life. The water rippled, distorting his dark image. The Spanish dancer rose to the ledge, collected the trilobite on her back, and conveyed him to the tide pool floor. There, he dismounted and nodded to each animal, addressing them by name. He turned to Siona, addressing her as Chordata's Daughter. Siona looked puzzled. *Chordata's Daughter? Who was Chordata, and where was she?*

The trilobite paused, gazed with his compound eyes across the tide pool toward the crashing waves, and then turned to Siona. The light of the sun glowed gold in the mosaic of over ten thousand hexagonal calcite lenses in each eye of the creature.

At this point in the story, we might expect to hear Siona's ultimate destiny that she, with only a primordial heart, would get her heart's desire to swim forever and never grow up. But whose story is really told before the last page is reached? Even if a story is told, it might not be the right one, especially if it is written or conveyed by a third party. There are so many ways that one can tell a tale. As the events unfold, we don't know what the trilobite said to Siona. Maybe the trilobite said Siona would remain a free being, unanchored to a rock; that her future would be of her choosing, unrestrained by her history and heritage. Perhaps he might have added how her descendants would swim freely through the sea and one day struggle to creep up on the land, breathing the air with relish and relief.

As centuries upon centuries passed, her descendants would walk the earth on two strong legs. They would harvest the inky mucus secretions from the hypobranchial glands of twelve thousand sea snails, close cousins of sea hares, and dye the trim of a cloth tunic dark purple, first calling the dye Tyrian purple—the color of kings and the blue-blooded, the color that gold could buy. And later, those creatures, those primates with the big brains, would discover the chemical composition and molecular structure of that very dye. The name of that dye would change from the fanciful to the matter-of-fact, and the chemist wearing the white labcoat would refer to the dye as 6,6'-dibromoindigo.

Those same primates would take their inspirations from the chemical prowess of the simple sponge, *Discodermia dissolute*, and after a lifetime of study, they too could formulate complex molecules, using a process called palladium-catalyzed cross-coupling. Mimicking the molecules made from sponges and squirts, they would make medicines to help their species battle grave diseases, such as cancer, when the proliferation of cells went amok, or Alzheimer's disease, when the very cells that made the mind went missing.

Far, far, far into the future, the great-grandchildren of the readers of this story would build strong but lightweight rocket ships based on the specialized proteins found in ragworm fangs, called Nvfp-1 (*Nereis virens fang protein -1*). Into deep space those creatures, still primates, would travel, forever curious about what they would discover next.

Or maybe the trilobite would tell Siona to brace up and face the facts. She was a sea squirt. It was her destiny to live as such and anchor her head to a rock, digest most of her brain and her lovely tail, and secrete that wondrous and tough tunic of cellulose. The idea that Siona would lose a good part of her brain and nervous system would likely cause her even more dismay, but that is what happens when squirts grow up. Perhaps the trilobite would also reflect on his own being and the future of the trilobites. Maybe the trilobite would sigh as he considered events in the future Permian extinction roughly 252 million years before you were born. He might contemplate that his kind would perhaps become nothing more than an imprint in stone—that his line was destined to first rise and then decline, following the trajectory of most species. Perhaps he also had some inkling that Siona's descendents would rise to rule for a brief chapter in the history of life. But maybe we can guess how the story went. If so, then this is how it was told.

"I know you are all tired and worn," said the trilobite. "Please eat and rest. Clarissa will tell you a story."

He snapped his antenna together, and a dozen tiny lobsterlike creatures appeared with red algae for Harold and tiny tasty morsels for Reilly and Sydney, carried on tiny shells in their slender claws. Their claws resembled miniature scissors. The leader of the tiny lobsterlike creatures was called Johnny and his identical twin brother was Edward. Collectively, they were known as the Lobsterish Ones. The Lobsterish Ones had brought nothing for Siona, as sea squirt larvae do not eat—a point that Siona certainly noted; she was not very hungry … yet. She settled down to rest on the sandy bottom of the new tide pool. She was eager to hear about her future.

"I will tell you a tale of that which is within," said Clarissa. Her voice was soft, but it carried well through the water. We already know now how fast and far sound travels in water.

"Harbored in each of you, in nearly all of your cells, are the instructions to make you who you are. Reilly harbors the instructions to make the brilliant and brave worm he has become. Harold holds the instructions to make the lovely, unique, and special sea hare that he is, complete with the finest voice and set of rhinophores to emerge to date in any tide pool, not to mention the ability to produce exceptionally tricky purple ink. Sydney has his own set of instructions that make him the wondrous orange star he is, with the fastest and strongest soon-to-be-controlled tube feet ever to touch the rocks and waterways of our tide pools, even though he has only four arms."

The creatures could not help but exchange satisfied looks with one another. Harold gazed at his rhinophores and swelled with pride. Sydney attempted to pump his tube feet, but they expanded—only on one side—with such force that he nearly flipped over. His hydraulics definitely needed some fine-tuning. Even Reilly took a quick glance down the length of his yellow body to admire (briefly) his segments and paddles.

"What about Siona?" asked the worm. "Does she have her own set of instructions too?"

"Oh, yes," replied the clam, stealing a glance at the trilobite. "Siona has the instructions to be a wondrous one-of-a-kind creature."

The trilobite stepped in and stopped at Clarissa's side. "What are those instructions in each of you? What are the instructions that make a creature a worm, hare, star, or squirt?" He paused, waiting for a reply that did not come. The trilobite went on. "It is what we call DNA, or deoxyribonucleic acid. I know that word might sound very strange to you—"

"What is deoxyribo ... stuff ... DNA good for?" interrupted Siona. "If I had some, could I keep my tail?"

"DNA harbors the code of life. It is the set of instructions, the blueprints, to make each of you what you are."

"Wait a minute," said Siona. "How can the same stuff make different creatures? This doesn't make any sense at all."

"Excellent question, Siona! Do you see those four piles of little snail shells over there?"

Siona looked in the direction that the trilobite pointed with his antennae and saw four piles of shells.

"Yes," said Siona, though she had no idea what snail shells had to do with DNA.

"Tell me what you see, Siona," said the trilobite.

"I see four piles of tiny snail shells. Each pile has its own color—gray, black, white, and brown."

The trilobite clicked its antennae again and conferred with Johnny, Edward, and the other Lobsterish Ones. The creatures used their slender claws to line up two rows of the gray (G), white (W), black (B), and brown (R) shells in what looked like random sequences on the sandy tide pool floor. In the first row the shells were lined up as:

G G G B B W B B B G G W B B W W B B R B W B W W B G

"Let's pretend that the first line is the code that makes you a sea squirt, Siona," said Clarissa, now moving forward by simply opening and closing her shell.

Siona looked at the line of shells. She knew she wasn't made out of shells. Maybe the clam was crazy and not clairvoyant after all. But the clam had saved them, so Siona thought it best to indulge the mollusk.

"And if you look at the second row, you will see a sequence that we can pretend is the code for Reilly the Ragworm," continued Clarissa.

Siona looked where the clam hovered. There below the first line of shells, the adroit Lobsterish Ones had made a second row of shells.

W B W B B B B R W W W R B G R W B W B G B

"What do you see, Siona?" asked the trilobite.

"I see two lines of shells in the sand at the bottom of the tide pool," said Siona.

"Tell me about the shells in the two lines."

Siona looked more closely. She saw that the two lines had a different number of shells; the first row had twenty-seven shells, and the second row had twenty-one shells. And she saw that each line had four different types of shells. Some were white, others black, and still others brown or gray. The numbers of shells and the sequence, or pattern, of the shells were different, yet the two lines were made of the same basic materials, or building blocks—that is, the shells. Siona relayed her observations to the trilobite, who nodded with only a hint of enthusiasm.

But Clarissa cried out, "Yes, yes! You got it!"

Siona was not sure what she had gotten. She still didn't know what the shells had to do with anything. So she ventured a question as politely as she could. "Clarissa," she said softly, "am I made of shells? I can see that the lines are both made up of shells, and each line is made of four different shell types. I can see that they have a different pattern, or sequence. But what does it mean?"

Clarissa turned slowly to face Siona. "It means a good deal, Siona. These aren't meant to represent a bunch of shells."

"They look a lot like shells," said Siona.

"Well, of course, they look like shells!" The clam smiled. "They are shells!"

Siona looked confused. Clarissa slowed down, speaking very slowly. "You are absolutely not made of shells, but you are made of widgets, or proteins. We are using the shells to represent the building blocks of DNA. DNA is like the musical score read by a conductor; it's the song in your cells that makes you a sea squirt—the notes, timing, beats, rhythm, and tune. Your sea squirt DNA conducts your cells to make sea squirt proteins at the right time, in the right place. My clam DNA conducts my cells to make clam proteins."

"Pro … proteins," stammered Siona, pausing for a moment. "Oh yes, I remember! The rotifers told me that proteins were like widgets that do stuff!" But still this was quite a bit of information for the young squirt to assimilate after hatching from an egg earlier that day and surviving her many ordeals.

Clarissa went on. "So how do we get from DNA to proteins? In our model of DNA using shells, there are four distinct units—a gray shell, a brown shell, a white shell, and a black shell." The clam paused, opening and closing her bivalve shell as if in brief meditation. "We have four separate units. What does this mean? Well, the way it works is that there is a secret code that is made out of three units of the DNA. For example, the first three shells in your line of shells are gray, gray, gray, and the first three shells in Reilly's line of shells are white, black, white. That means that your DNA codes are for different protein building blocks than Reilly's DNA. The DNA code is in units of three. And they code for specific protein building blocks. And the regions of DNA that code for proteins are called genes. Look—see what the Lobsterish Ones have done."

The Lobsterish Ones had sorted more shells in groups of three. Using their long, thin claws like the styli of ancient scribes, Johnny and Edward wrote the letters of the alphabet in the sand right next to the triplet codon of shells.

One can take comfort in the alphabet; it's something learned in kindergarten. But had the Lobsterish Ones been molecular biologists, rather than using shells, they would have been very comfortable using the four basic building blocks of DNA—that wondrous molecule of life, passed from one generation to the next since the beginnings of biological history. Like the writings on an ancient scroll, life's history is etched into the very sequences of these four simple building blocks in a quaternary script or code, much as life's history is also recorded in fossils etched in stone. Rather than using shells of black, brown, white, and gray, the molecular biologist, with pipette in hand, would call out with glee and passion, "Adenine, thymine, guanine, and cytosine!"

Well, after learning the alphabet, this young molecular biologist would learn that there was a secret code in the DNA, a codon. And the codons, or sequences of three of the four DNA building blocks, would code for one of the twenty amino acids, the building blocks of proteins. So that in the lab, the molecular biologist would call out to the protein chemist. The protein chemist would look up from her microcentrifuge tubes and reply by calling out the names of each of the twenty amino acids: "Alanine, cysteine, aspartic acid, glutamic acid, phenylalanine, glycine, histidine, isoleucine, lysine, leucine, methionine, asparagine, proline, glutamine, arginine, serine, threonine, valine, tryptophan, and tyrosine, and that is the stuff of which we are made."

And the molecular biologist and protein chemist would share a smile, reach for their pipettes and test tubes, and continue with their experiments. So yes, the Lobsterish Ones, using their claws like styli, wrote the letters of the alphabet next to the shells as shown below.

BBB	= A
BWB	= B
BRB	= C
BGB	= D
BBW	= E
BWW	= F
BRW	= G
BGW	= H
BRB	= I
BRW	= J
BRR	= K

BRG   = L
BGB   = M
BGW   = N
BGR   = O
BGG   = P
WBB   = Q
WBW   = R
GGG   = S
WBG   = T
WWB   = U
WWW   = V
WWR   = W
WWG   = X
WRB   = Y
WRG   = Z

"So, Siona," said the clam, "use the code above to figure out what this spells."

(GGG)(BBW)(BBB) (GGG)(WBB)(WWB)(BRB)(WBW)(WBG)

Siona spelled it out (because in this story, sea squirts can spell):

S E A   S Q U I R T

"Wonderful!" cried the clam, clapping with her bivalve shell. Clarissa then moved to the second line of shells. "Now use the code to figure out what this spells."

(WBW) (BBB) (BRW) (WWR) (BGR) (WBW) (BGB)

Siona spelled it out:

R A G W O R M

"Excellent! Excellent work!" cried Clarissa. "Please keep in mind that I am only a mollusk, and my model of how DNA translates to protein has been simplified. The real protein building blocks are called amino acids, but I prefer to use the alphabet since it is easier for our young readers to understand. I suspect that they will be introduced to the correct terminology in high school."

"Our readers?" asked Siona, very puzzled, "What are they?"

"Well, spell out this next code to find out who our readers are," suggested the clam.

(BGW)(WWB)(BGB)(BBB)(BGW) (BWB)(BBW)(BRB)(BGW)(BRW)(GGG)

So Siona spelled:

HUMAN   BEINGS

"Hmmm," said Siona, "I've never heard of these creatures. Are they like us?"

The trilobite stepped forward. "Yes, Siona. They are very much like you, yet very different too."

Siona stared up at the trilobite. "I am sorry," she said. "I still don't understand. How can creatures be both the same yet different too?" She looked from the segmented worm to the four-armed star and from the blob-like hare to the armored trilobite. Clarissa opened her shell in a pastel display of mother of pearl. Dancer flapped her brightly colored frill-like parapodia. Siona glanced at her tail and gave it a wiggle. She was the only one that had a tail.

The creatures were different, yet their gadgetry to generate energy, sense their surroundings, and propagate was nearly the same. It was as if new and alternative features were built on top of the basics. Later, the primates with the big brains would work to unravel the mystery of DNA in themselves and other creatures, searching for commonalities and departures and connections and deviations in the sequence of DNA to discover how creation might fit together in the grand experiment of life—a journey started more than a billion years ago, with the chance of marching millions of years into the future.

There was a long pause. Siona continued to stare at the trilobite.

The trilobite held her gaze and stepped forward. He came very close to the young squirt, towering above her like a black fortress. Siona looked up into the eyes of the trilobite. She saw her image reflected again and again, more than twenty thousand times over in the tiny calcite lenses of the mosaic eyes.

"You have something to say, don't you, Siona?" he asked in a gentle whisper.

"Yes, I guess I do," said Siona. "Is it okay if I don't understand?"

"Yes, Siona," replied the trilobite. "On the stage of life, each creature has its entrance and exit." The trilobite looked to the sun, catching the light in his mosaic eyes. "Creatures—like you, Siona—change the cast of characters in the scenes that follow."

Siona shook her head and looked down at the three rows of shells, each a different sequence, each representing a different being. "What if …" she said, "what if I could change my DNA sequence? With a few changes, my sequence might look like Reilly's, and maybe I could keep my tail."

A change could be as simple as guanine accidentally swapped for adenine or a thymine accidentally deleted. On a grander scale, whole hunks of viral DNA might be inserted, or a piece of DNA copied one too many times, or even lost in the shuffle during cell division. And whether this would be bad or good was all a function of fate. Chance. Luck.

"Maybe," Siona continued, "I could change things just enough to keep on swimming. Could that happen?"

"Chordata's Daughter," said the trilobite, addressing Siona again, "you have your code. You have a life." The trilobite pointed up with one of his antenna. There above them, sparkling like stars, were hundreds and hundreds of sea squirt eggs. From the eggs, new larvae emerged. The broken eggs turned to tiny prisms from which erupted ribbons of color, like fireworks at the surface of the water.

The little larvae sang out loud. "Look at us; we finally hatched!" They sang to their parents. They danced and frolicked in the warm waters. "We need to find a rock," they chanted. The words they spoke were a bit different, but the tune was familiar.

> Find a rock
> Find a rock
> A place to dock,
> Time is ticking in our clock.
> A rock, a rock is what we need.
> To our DNA we heed.

"Tell me, Siona. What do you see?" asked the trilobite, his voice barely audible above the songs of the squirts and the waves crashing at the far side of the pool.

Siona looked at the new life dancing above. "I see the first chapter of my life," whispered Siona. She pivoted to view the baby squirts. A couple of new squirts were batting a diatom back and forth with their tails. The diatom was laughing with near hysterics as he collided with one tiny tail, only to bounce off another.

"Oh! Yippee! Yikes. Whoa!" cried the diatom. Other young larvae continued singing their little songs, touching their heads briefly to stones and rocks, searching for the best rock possible.

The four newcomers were silent, watching the baby squirts. Siona saw the white sea squirt parents gaze with beatific smiles at their new brood. "Ah, the beauty of our little darlings! The beauty of our little squirts," the parents said in unison.

"They are so lovely. Lovely," said Reilly, watching the new beings dancing above in jubilation.

7

The Battle of Shrimp and Worm

RIDING ON THE DRUM BEAT rhythm of the waves, the young squirts sang their song, adding to the ongoing improvisation, guided and driven by the percussion of waves pounding on rock: *kaboom*, followed by the treble of splashing water droplets—splish, splash, dribble, ping, ping—and the whooshing of water back to the sea. Kaboom! Splish, splash, dribble, ping, ping. A long whoosh. Kaboom! Adding to the percussion, the bacrites splashed at the surface of the water in their long, straight shells. The male *Wiwaxia* beat their broad spines together. "Bang … bang. Bang … bang." The female *Wiwaxia* went "Hum … hum, hum, hum. Hum … hum, hum, hum." And the *Hallucigenia* tapped their long spines together—"tap, tap, tap." And then there was the *tick, tick, tick* of the proto-barnacles and the flutelike songs of the tiny rotifers, gleeful for their widgets within.

So it took some time for the creatures to process the *click*, the sound that sliced through the melody. It cut deep through the water. It was just a sound, a noise. How could a simple sound embody the essence of evil or an impending tragedy? But that *click* was like the cocking of a gun. A veil of dread descended over the tide pool. The baby squirts hesitated in their play. The adult squirts squinted, searching for the source of their fears. Those that could clamped their shells shut. The Lobsterish Ones curled into tiny balls. The snails squeezed their bodies into compressed spirals. All but one clam dug down deep into the sand. The tide pool grew quiet with only the drumming of the surf keeping time.

The rhinophores of the hare stood on end. He shuddered, and a tiny puff of a purple cloud emerged slightly to the right of the sea hare. Harold looked horrified as he watched the miniscule puff of purple ink drifting away, until it was so diluted it disappeared. He was still trembling when Siona swam to him.

"What's wrong, Harold?" she asked. "Are you trying to make more ink?"

Harold nodded, his rhinophores flapping with near hysterics. "I just can't seem to squeeze out anymore ink!" he wailed. "It's all petered out! It is my only trick, and I can't muster more than a teeny-weeny puff!" Looking at the young squirt, he regained a bit of his composure. "It's crossed my mind to ask the trilobite if there might be a way to make more ink. Maybe I can change my DNA too."

They did not have time to continue their discussion. A loud *crack* was followed by a *snap* and a horrible *hiss*. The shockwave hit Siona, and she tumbled over and over, hitting the sandy bottom. Above her, dozens of new squirts, caught in the direct line of the supersonic bubbles, began falling like confetti. The screams and cries of the still-living young squirts were deafening.

Above Siona, the pistol shrimp lowered his enormous pistol claw, skewering the falling squirts with his bayonet claw. His armored plates shone bronze in the setting sun. From each segmented plate rose a series of spines. The shrimp drifted down with the falling squirts. Into his mouth he stuffed those dead and dying. He smacked. His stomach bulged. He took aim again with his pistol claw. Siona heard the sharp *click*, *snap*, and *hiss*. There was a flash of bright orange as Sydney shielded Siona's body with his. The shockwave struck the star, knocking him over onto his back. His tube feet pumped the water. With his underside exposed, the star was in grave danger. Harold slid as fast as his belly would take him. He leaned over the star as Siona tried to push the star right side up with her head.

"Sydney! Grab my rhinophores and pull!"

The star was under the pistol shrimp. Siona stared at Sydney's pumping feet. She looked back up at the shrimp, then to Harold, and then back to the pumping feet. "Wait—I have a plan. It's really risky, but I think it might work," she whispered to the star and hare. "It will mean getting all your feet under control," she said to the star. "Remember what happened when Harold fell from the lava tube, and he landed on top of you?" With her brain cells firing, she told them her plan.

"It's our only chance," said the hare, and he slithered his way across as many of those tube feet as he could until he was right on top of the wiggling orange star. "Oh, I hope my ink will work. Oh, I hope my ink will work!"

"Sydney, stop wiggling," cried Siona. "You need to control as many feet as you can!"

The star tried to calm himself. Two hundred twenty-two tube feet contracted. The other feet were out of control, but for the second time since he became a four-armed star, Sydney was in control of the majority.

Siona heard the surviving sea squirt larvae crying. She saw their parents holding their heads and covering their eyes with their siphons.

"*Help! Help!*" cried the sea squirt parents. "Our babies! Our brood! "

Siona saw a mother sea squirt trying to pry herself from her rock to get to her babies. Siona swam to the frightened tiny creatures—a group of about fifty had survived the first assaults. They were dazed and stunned. "Babies, follow me!" Siona yelled. Some shook their heads, their eyes blinking in disbelief. "I'm a sea squirt larva too!" Siona said. "I just have a big tail! I'm here to help you!"

There was another volley of supersonic bubbles. Siona could feel the heat. She circled around the frightened larvae, rounding them up with her tail. Sweeping by the adult squirts, Siona led the babies to safety behind the small rock fortress. "Stay here," she told them, trying to control her own fears. "It will be okay." To her relief, Clarissa was at her side, just as the clam had been in the black lava tube. And the clam was very calm.

"Siona, stay here with the baby squirts," said Clarissa. "You need to stay behind these rocks where it is safe."

Siona peered around the rocks. At the far side of the tide pool, closest to the open ocean, there were about half a dozen larvae. All but the biggest squirt looked terrified. Siona could see the other five trembling, first darting one way and then another. Beyond the larvae were three small rocks. The rocks barely rose above the surface of the sandy bottom. But they could offer the necessary protection.

"I might be able to get them to those tiny rocks," Siona stated, more to herself than to the clam. She felt a tug on her tail and looked behind. Clarissa was holding her tail tightly between her bivalve shells.

"Clarissa, what are you doing? Let me go," cried Siona.

Between clenched shells Clarissa mumbled, "Siona, we need you here. You need to stay safe."

Above the pair there was a rumble, and the water swirled. Siona looked up to see Reilly swimming full speed ahead toward the wayward babies, like a bright and brilliant yellow submarine. "I'll get them," was all he said as he sped past.

"No, Reilly, *no!*" cried Siona, trying to pull her tail free from Clarissa's grip. "They won't understand." She heard cries of terror from her kind.

"Not a ragworm and pistol shrimp again!" cried the sea squirt adults in unison.

Siona twisted her tail, and, wiggling, she freed herself from Clarissa's grip. She raced to catch up with Reilly. With the yellow ragworm approaching, five of the six baby squirts screamed, and two raced away.

"I think he is trying to help us," said the larger squirt with bright orange stripes along his sides.

"That's right; that's right," said Siona, catching the two escapees and rounding them up with her tail. "Look! Go there," she said to the wayward squirts, pointing to the three rocks where Reilly had escorted three of the trembling creatures and the larger squirt with bright orange stripes. With the six larvae together again, the worm motioned with his paddles that they should hide low in the cracks of the rocks.

"Thank you!" they cried. "You are very nice for a ragworm."

Reilly nearly smiled. Siona nodded in agreement. They were at the far end of the tide pool. Clumps of algae, green and lush, grew behind their hiding place. A wall of black rock rose beyond the algae, separating the pool from the ocean beyond. Occasionally, wet fingers from the ocean reached over the wall of stone, touching and swirling the calm waters of the pool, only to retreat back to the sea, like an unwanted guest at a private party.

In the middle of the tide pool, the pistol shrimp was casually eating. A dozen lifeless larvae were skewered like shish kebab at the end of his bayonet claw. "Delicious, simply delicious." The pistol shrimp smacked with his mouth full. "I'm so full that I can barely eat another bite."

But the shrimp continued to eat.

A nightmarish *Hallucigenia*, with long red spines, raced on its fourteen clawed legs through a curtain of algae to the mighty shrimp. Siona thought the creature must be one of Helamite's cousins. The shrimp laughed. He aimed. He fired. The blast of the supersonic bubbles severed the algae neatly in half and struck the nightmarish creature, breaking three of its strong spines. The animal tumbled in the turbulent waters, rolling, and falling on its back. Its remaining spines were stuck deep in the sand, and the creature's clawed legs flailed in the water. The shrimp fired again. The nightmarish creature slumped deeper in the sand and did not move again, its legs missing.

"Now maybe I can eat in peace," said the shrimp, burping between bites, "though I can barely eat another bite."

From the colony of the squirts, a new brood of eggs bobbed in the water. The sun shone on the starry eggs. In the egg-locked larvae, little clocks tick-tock-ticked, without making a sound, triggering their untimely debut. Out of the eggs the new brood of sea squirt larvae hatched, silver and shiny, singing their wee songs, unaware of the danger. The shrimp, his stomach round and full, stopped chewing. He watched the new larvae.

"I could use some target practice," mused the shrimp, aiming his pistol claw.

"What cruel creature would use another living thing for target practice?" cried Reilly. "Siona, we can't let that happen."

"Reilly, do you think you could get the new larvae to that big rock where the others are hiding right over there?" Siona asked, pointing with her tail to the rock citadel beyond the sea squirt adults.

"I can do it," said the worm, "but it would help if there were some sort of distraction."

"Okay!" cried Siona, and she sped from behind the rocks, ignoring Reilly's frantic call. She swam to the pistol shrimp. "Hey, you stupid, dumb shrimp! I bet you can't hit me! Na, na-na, na-na, nah," taunted Siona.

There was a group gasp from the sea squirt colony, and through their collective connectivity they simultaneously covered their eyes with their siphons. The shrimp turned to face Siona. Reilly grimaced and bolted from behind the rocks. He used his body like a moving corral and began to herd the new larvae to the rock fortress, but there were many that he could not reach. He sighed and continued to herd those he could to safety. With a flash of red the young red ragworm raced forward, sweeping up the larvae that Reilly had been forced to leave behind. Together, the two worms brought the new larvae to safety behind the wall of the rock fortress with the others.

The shrimp laughed. "Who is the dumb and stupid one now?" he said, taking aim at Siona.

Siona used her mighty tail and her widgets within. Straight up she streaked, with her tail beating, her heart pounding. She breached the surface of the water, escaping into the air as the supersonic bubbles burst harmlessly below. Without wings, Siona fell, tumbling back into the water. She did not know how fast a pistol shrimp could reload. The water turned to fire. Siona cried in the searing heat. A lone shield of white and pastel mother of pearl blocked the burning water. Clarissa's shell clamped shut, and Siona was thrown into darkness. Together they tumbled, striking a rock. Clarissa's shell fell open. Siona heard the shrimp laugh.

"Time to blast that old clam out of her shell," snorted the shrimp.

"Clarissa," sobbed Siona, "I'm so sorry. I didn't want to put you in danger!"

The shrimp took aim with his gun-like claw. Siona cringed. A black cloud descended, dark and heavy as a shroud, covering Clarissa and Siona.

"Close your shell now," said the trilobite to the clam.

The supersonic bubbles exploded on the midnight-black segments, pitting the sand all around as the trilobite covered Clarissa and Siona with his massive body. Siona peered out from under the trilobite's segments between a set of armored legs. From behind the black rock fortress, Siona saw the yellow worm emerge, his eyes red.

"The inside-out, upside-down circle," she said to herself, gazing at the first dozen of the worm's paddles on each side of his brilliant yellow body. "That's it!" she cried, using her tail to write the equation in the sand. "I have to tell Reilly! It's the mean turbulent kinetic energy of the flow! Why didn't I see that before?"

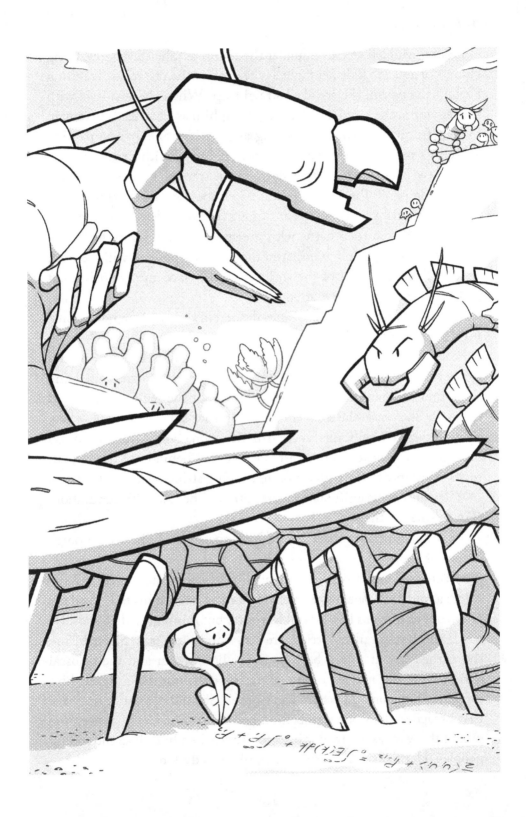

Siona wiggled free from under the trilobite. She stayed low, using clumps of algae to hide her flight as she sped to the ragworm. Traveling beyond the worm, she streaked straight up. When she was level with the ragworm, she raced from behind, using him as a barricade to remain hidden from the shrimp for as long as possible. She arrived panting at Reilly's head and whispered her idea, pointing with her tail first to Reilly's twelfth paddle and then down to the star and hare at the bottom of the tide pool. The star now held 235 tube feet, nicely compressed under the squishy body of the hare. Siona reminded Reilly of what they had learned from their battle with the spiders—that armor had weak spots at the hinges and joints. And there, Siona pointed with her tail, right before the barrel of the shrimp's pistol claw, the armored joint looked—if not weak—less strong.

The ragworm nodded. His fangs flashed in the sun. "Go now, Siona. Find a rock and hide."

Siona sighed, annoyed by the great irony. She seemed to need a rock even while she still swam free. The large rock fortress shielding the scores of new squirt larvae was closer, but the path was bare and exposed. She chose the smaller rocks at the far side of the pool, where the half dozen other squirt larvae still hid. Siona bolted from one patch of algae to the next, until at last she scurried behind the three small rocks. The large squirt with the orange racing stripes glanced at her tail.

"That is one beautiful tail you have there," he said with admiration. "I'm Bernie, by the way."

"Oh, ni-ni-nice to meet you," said Siona. "I … I like those orange stripes of yours."

"You do?" asked Bernie with surprise. "The white squirts call my colors a mutation, but you're blue!" He looked back at his tail. "And my tail is not as quite as long or full as yours, but it is bigger than most."

"I think your tail and stripes are very handsome," said Siona, before she turned her attention back to the yellow worm and the colossal shrimp. She did not see Bernie blink his eyes, nor did she hear him exclaim, "Someone thinks I'm handsome!" She did not notice the wave that breached the stone wall behind her either. She barely noticed the pull of the wave as it retreated back to the sea, bending algae and rolling pebbles. Her focus was on the worm, his eyes dark red.

"I think it is time for you to leave," said Reilly to the shrimp.

The pistol shrimp laughed. He shook his armor and pointed his giant claw directly at the bright yellow worm.

He snorted. "Don't you worms ever give up?"

"No," said Reilly. And he charged to the shrimp, staring down the biological barrel of a gun and racing toward an unknown outcome. But surely he must have known the odds were against him. The shrimp was that much larger and stronger. At any moment, the shrimp would release the trigger, and the bubbles would explode, hissing and horrible. The shrimp cocked his claw. Seconds counted now; luck counted now. The worm dove deep. A flurry of brown circles and rhinophores rose right where the worm had been, followed by a miniscule puff of purple ink. It was barely enough to make a baby sea squirt sneeze, but it was enough to distract the shrimp. In one moment, the shrimp was looking into the red eyes of a yellow worm, and in the next, there was a sea hare rolling and tumbling right in the line of fire.

"Where is that blasted worm now?" bellowed the shrimp. "And how can a sea hare swim?"

The wiggling feet of the star caught his attention, as the sea hare sank through the water. The shrimp laughed loudly and, looking down, aimed his deadly claw at the sea hare and star. "No more fun and games for you two fools," he said, still laughing.

Above the shrimp, Reilly sailed through the apex of an inside-out, upside-down circle. His fangs opened wide as he plunged toward the shrimp. On each side of the worm, the first dozen paddles were pressed tight against his body. The worm held his course with fatal execution. At the moment of impact, there was a bang, followed by a resounding *crack* as the fangs of the worm found a weak spot in the armor of the shrimp. The fangs closed with a snap, severing the giant claw from its master. The bubbles dissipated harmlessly with a long hiss. The severed claw of the shrimp cocked and clicked, opening and closing as it floated to the sandy floor of the tide pool.

The pistol shrimp cried out. For the first time in the history of the known universe, a worm had completed the elusive inside-out, upside-down circle. That same worm was equipped with fangs laced and hardened with extra zinc and cross-linked proteins. That worm also had new knowledge of what was weak in the armor of spiders and shrimps, a fact brought to his attention by a tiny sea squirt.

The hapless shrimp watched his great claw flounder on the tide pool floor. "So you happened to get lucky, did you?" screamed the shrimp to the worm. "You *really* think that you can take *me* down, you freakish little worm, along with your pesky friends?" The shrimp laughed. "I will save you for last! Now where is that silly sea hare of yours?"

"I am right down here," said Harold, "right where any normal hare should be."

"Normal, yes indeed!" screamed the shrimp. "What's wrong with that four-armed star of yours? Is he going to lie around on his back all day and let the rest of us have all this fun without him?" Sydney's tube feet pumped wildly. The shrimp raised his remaining bayonet claw, stabbing the water. "I am going to run you two through and through."

The shrimp dove, with the bayonet claw leading the way. Reilly plunged too, swimming under the shrimp, arching his back, ready to rise above. But the shrimp had lived a long time; he twisted in the water, focused on the worm, with his bayonet blazing in the sun. Reilly passed the apex of another inside-out, upside-down circle. He rammed the shrimp, pushing the massive creature to the 235 tube feet, tight as coils, waiting below. With a deft movement, the shrimp struck with his bayonet, piercing the water and the worm. The bayonet cut the ragworm between the hearts pounding in the sixth and seventh segments. It was as if the wind was knocked out of the worm. Withdrawing his blade, the shrimp flicked his tail, speeding his own descent but casting the worm to the far side of the tide pool. Reilly hit the rock wall just beyond where Siona and Bernie hid. As for the shrimp, he landed square on the star's many feet. The tube feet expanded in unison, 235 strong, catapulting the shrimp out of the tide pool and onto the rocks above.

The colony of sea squirts cheered, moving their siphons like pom-poms. Four Lobsterish Ones captured the severed pistol claw, holding it high. They paraded with the severed claw to the cheering of the squirts. The squirt larvae emerged from behind the rock fortress and joined in the parade.

Reilly watched the parade from below the surface as a slow smile spread across his face, with his fangs arching perfectly.

"You did it! You did it!" cried Siona to the worm. Reilly replied with a weak smile. Siona turned to watch the parade of the pistol claw.

Bernie bumped Siona with his head. "Let's go join the others," he said.

Siona flicked her tail and turned back to Reilly. She squinted at the worm and gasped when she saw the wounds—gaping holes from top to bottom, from ventral to dorsal between the sixth and seventh segments. Siona cried out, racing to Reilly. Before her, a frothing wave hurtled over the rock wall where the worm floated. The wave rolled the worm, turning him as if inspecting what value the worm might still possess. The wave shrugged. With its inspection complete, the wave fled back to the sea and carried Reilly in its watery grip, out of the tide pool and into the open ocean.

*   *   *

"*No! No!*" screamed Siona the human, jumping from the rocking chair. "That can't happen. Please! You have to undo that right now! You have to untell it. You can't let the wave take Reilly away! The ocean is too … too big … and fierce, like a monster, with things that grab your legs and hold you down so you can't breathe, no matter how hard you try."

"Like a monster? The sea?" Siona's mother paused and whispered, "Siona, the first matter and manner of life came from the sea. That's what we are, all of us, all saltwater and grit."

"Then why don't I have gills?" Siona asked. She covered her face with her hands. "You weren't there, Mom. You are always around when I don't need you, and when I do need you, you aren't there. Just like with the snake and that green car!"

"What did I miss? When wasn't I there when you needed me?"

Siona started to cry. She wiped her nose with the back of her hand. "I have something to say," she sobbed. "Something I need to tell you."

Siona's mother leaned forward, elbows on her knees, her brow creased. "What? What? Tell me! Please!"

"But when I tell you," Siona cried to the ceiling, "you'll leave me for what you love the most, and I'll still be all alone!"

"Siona, please tell me what happened."

"Okay, I'll tell you now," said Siona.

And Siona was back on the beach. She and Gracie Alice had completed the moat around the sand castle. Gracie Alice's little brother dug a deep pit to provide the castle residents with a lake. Three other children were busy completing the path of pebbles from the castle to the lake. Gracie Alice's older cousin bent down to pick up a shell in the surf, her long hair dropping to the water. They were there for the annual departmental retreat with the other children, the near descendants of the marine biology faculty. There was one older boy, a foot taller than the others, whose father had spent a career on one fossil rock. With Gracie Alice's cousin and the older boy as chaperones, the children had escaped the tedium of the adult debate on the origins of the Ediacaran tubular fossils of the Onega Peninsula.

With the sand castle finished, Siona said, "Oh, let's go there"— she pointed—"on those rocks." And the children scurried like insects, making a sport of jumping from rock to rock, their sport carrying them closer to the ending of the rocks and the beginning of the sea. There the sea pounded, striking high and lifting white into the air. The children could feel the spray.

Gracie Alice stopped on the wet rocks. "The rocks are getting slippery, Siona," she said, holding her little brother by his elbow. Gracie Alice's cousin stood in advance of the other children, blocking their approach to the sea.

Siona glanced down the jetty of wet rocks. A flash of silver caught her eye. It wiggled; it had a tail. It had fins. Siona pointed. "That fish needs help," she said. "You stay here, and I'll be right back." She took off and jumped from one rock to another, ignoring the protests of the others. She slipped on a clump of kelp, bruising her knee on the rock.

"Forget about that darn fish!" called the older boy.

Gracie Alice's cousin called, "That's far enough now. Come back."

Siona did not stop until she reached the rock where the fish flapped. The rock was streaked with the passing of birds. A lone gull flew with a mussel caught in its beak, rising high in the air above the rock. The gull opened its beak, and the mussel fell, striking the stone at

Siona's feet. The shell broke; the mussel oozed. The gull cried overhead. Siona winced. Stepping over the broken shell, she reached for what she could still save—the fish—and clutched it in her hands. Cooing to the creature, she carried it down to the water's edge, to the sea swirling below. With a gentle underhand toss, she volleyed the fish back home. The water's rings that marked the return of the fish disappeared with the surge of the sea. Siona waved to her friends as she scrambled back up the wet rocks.

She heard thunder from the sea, and Gracie Alice screamed. Siona turned back to face the sea. *Is there something wrong with the fish?* she wondered. Above her, a wave towered. Siona heard Gracie Alice scream again. The wave crashed, swallowing Siona, rolling her into the frothy water. Ropes of kelp caught her legs and waist, wrapping around her neck, tying her down. Seaweed laced with scum whipped her face. She kicked, trying to force her freedom. Her hands slapped the sea. But the beast that was the water made no move to surrender. Siona grabbed the kelp between her fingers, yanking it from her legs, body, and neck. She was free from the kelp. The ocean surged, pushing Siona from the shore, holding her captive, like a cat with a mouse—the unintentional consequences of nature.

Siona panicked. She could taste it; panic was salty, like blood. She could hear panic; it was the sound of the belching, roaring bowels of some giant monster, and she the meat to be digested. She could feel panic; it was the heavy pressure of the water. She could see panic; it was the sight of kelp, like rope-thin, narrow men grown dark green in the sea. Anchored by their narrow legs to the sand below, they jerked in the flow of ocean. Holding her breath, Siona could not scream. *There must be an up. Where is up? And air? And air? There—where the dark gray is morphing to light gray. The light. It's lighter there.* She followed, positively phototactic. Her arms straight over her head, as if hoping for lungs in her fingertips. She breached the surface, gulping air. She could not call out. She tried but only gurgled. Her hands danced on the surface of the water. The water rose, and she slipped under again. She kicked her feet, pushing her nose and mouth above the water, gulping air. The weight of her body pulled her head under. She could see her fingers above the water, as if through a darkening tunnel. The tunnel narrowed. There was only a small circle of blue. She saw her hands in the circle, waving and fluttering. *If I were that fish*, thought Siona, *this would not be happening.* The tunnel went dark, as if someone had turned out the lights. *My mom and dad are going to be very angry with me.*

Under her arms, large hands gripped her body, hoisting her up out of the water. She landed face down on a surfboard, rocking in the waves. She coughed a waterfall of water. Hands pressed on her back. Water escaped from her nose. She coughed again and rolled onto her back. Wispy clouds hovered in a deep blue sky, their edges brushed in gold. An arm held her head as another wave rolled, carrying them closer to shore. Siona put her hand in the hand of the man, her knuckles white. The water stilled. Her panic eased. The hand held her firm. The board moved to shore.

The man was talking. Her name? "Siona. I think it might be Siona," she heard herself say. Siona closed her eyes, breathing air—lovely, miraculous air. She heard Gracie Alice call her name. There was the shore again. The beach. The man, a surfer, dark in his wetsuit, stood beside her on the board, waist deep in water. He lifted her, cradling her in his arms, and carried her to shore.

"You must be a god," mused Siona.

"You must be lucky," was the god's reply. He shook his head, the water's spray a halo.

On the beach, Gracie Alice's cousin wrapped Siona in a towel. Gracie Alice held Siona tight. The surfer god returned to his board and the sea.

"And this," said Siona to Gracie Alice and the others, "will have to be our secret. No one can ever say a word about this, ever." Siona stared out to the sea at what she had once loved and what her mother loved best. It would break her mother's heart to know that the sea could cause so much harm. Siona hung her head and sobbed.

And she was back, standing on the carpet in front of her mother. Her mother rocked in the rocking chair.

"I hate the sea. I hate it. It scares me so much!" Siona cried, still staring up at the ceiling. "I'm sorry. I'm not brave like Siona the Sea Squirt. I'm not the daughter you want me to be."

Siona's mother stopped rocking.

"And you'll leave me for what you love the most. I'll be all alone." Siona trembled. Tears fell from her cheeks. "It's what you love the most—the sea. The ocean and all that slime you collect." She clenched her fists.

Siona's mother rose from the chair and held her daughter tight. "It's you I love the most. You. More than the deepest part of any of the oceans. More than anything else in the universe." She stepped back, still holding Siona. "Look at me," she said, wiping the tears from Siona's checks. "It's you I love the most."

Siona sobbed, leaning into her mother. Without saying another word Siona's mother pulled her daughter onto the rocking chair. Siona felt her mother's arms close around her, warding off the demons and sea monsters lurking in the room and in her memory. And she was rocking on her granddaddy's great big rocking chair.

"They better save that worm," whispered Siona.

8

The Portal and Luciferase

"REILLY, REILLY!" SIONA SCREAMED AT the rock wall. She sped away but whirled back around, gaining speed. "I'm coming, Reilly. I'm coming to get you." Reaching the rock wall, she swam straight up. With a mighty swish of her tail, she breached the surface of the water, soaring into the air. The rock towered above. Siona fell back into the water, tumbling to the sand below. The Lobsterish Ones, holding the severed claw, stopped their march. The sea squirts waved their siphons, squinting their eyes.

"Siona, what happened?" cried Sydney, tubing his way over to her. Not far behind, Harold slithered, his rhinophores straining forward. Bernie raced after Sydney and Harold, catching them in no time.

Siona lay on her side in the sand. "Reilly is gone. A wave grabbed him and carried him off."

"A wave? Oh, that's nothing for a worm like Reilly," said the star.

"I'm sure he will be back in no time at all," said Harold, panting.

Siona cried to the sand. "No, no. I'm sorry, Reilly. I'm so sorry!"

"It was just a wave," said Sydney. "Reilly knows how to ride a wave, even a big one. He'll be fine."

Bernie tapped Siona with the tip of his tail. "Do you have something you need to tell us? What"—Bernie looked up at the rock wall, his orange racing stripes gold in the sun—"happened to Reilly?"

Siona sobbed.

"Siona, is there something you need to tell us?" Bernie asked again.

"The pistol shrimp!" wailed Siona. "The pistol shrimp hurt Reilly—stabbed him with his bayonet claw. He has a wound that cut him all the way through!" Siona sobbed so hard that bright-blue nanoscale whiskers in a cellulose blend dripped from the tip of her head to the sand below.

"What?" cried Sydney, his tube feet pumping. Harold slumped; his rhinophores drooped.

On the back of the dancer rode the trilobite and Clarissa the Clam. Clarissa rolled from Dancer's undulating back and came to a rest at Siona's side.

"Siona," whispered the clam—a dark crack showed on her bright-white shell—"life is abundantly given and taken away. We are fortunate to have known such a brilliant worm."

Siona stared at the crack in the clam's shell.

"Listen to that," said the trilobite, sliding onto the sand. The colony of adult sea squirts and all the sea squirt larvae were singing and chanting.

"Reilly, Reilly, the king of the worms. Four cheers for the yellow worm!" The Lobsterish Ones raised their claws like batons, conducting the great choir of squirts. "Was ever a worm so worthy? Cheers for Reilly! Cheers for the worm! Praise be the hearts of that splendid worm!"

"He'll be back," said Harold. "He's a very strong worm."

But Clarissa the Clairvoyant Clam shook her damaged shell. "Lost. Lost," was all that she could mutter to the sand below.

Siona rose from the tide pool floor and wiggled, shaking the sand from her tiny body. "I'm going after him. He rescued me from the sponge and the spiders. Now it's my turn. I'm going to use my nanoscale whiskers and cellulose blend to fix him and bring him back."

"Siona," cried Clarissa, trembling, "you have to be where it is safe. You need to stay alive. Now that you have your nanoscale whiskers, you have to find a rock soon. There is no time! So much more than you know is at stake!"

"Well, if I can't find a rock, then I guess I'll have to keep swimming forever." Siona paused and then said, "For the rest of my life."

"Siona, if you go to the open ocean," said Clarissa, "you surely would swim for what would be the rest of your life!" The clam cried.

The trilobite moved to the clam. A black antenna reached across the broken shell. Clarissa grew quiet and still.

"Is Reilly still alive?" Siona asked the clairvoyant clam.

Clarissa opened her shell. Brilliant light chiseled through the crack in her shell, striking the mother of pearl. "Yes, but he is weak ..."

Harold sobbed. "He had such a unique scent. Like courage and metal," the hare lamented, his rhinophores drooping.

"Like mettle?" asked Siona.

"Yes, like metal," replied the hare.

"And you remember his scent?"

"Oh yes, of course," said Harold. "We hares have a wonderful olfactory memory. So of course I remember that Reilly had a most magnificent scent."

"No, Harold," cried Siona, "he *has* a magnificent scent!" She opened her eyes wide. Harold opened his eyes wide too, his rhinophores bolting straight up. He blinked. Siona blinked.

"Maybe," ventured Harold, "maybe I could find Reilly—track him down. Follow the scent molecules."

Siona nodded. Her eyes opened wider, and then she shook her head, frowning. "I know you could do it, Harold. Those rhinophores of yours are so special and magnificent. But it would be too risky."

Harold bit his left rhinophore. "Too risky? *Risky?* Remember he saved us all from those spiders. I am going to help you find him. I only need to find one scent molecule, one in a billion, and I can find him. Maybe I can adjust the sensitivity of my systems and detect one molecule in a trillion. And we could ride down the path of molecules until we find Reilly." The hare paused a moment and then said, "And then I would know for sure that my rhinophores are as special as we believe."

"And," said the star, "if Harold is going, then so am I. He'll need me to hold him onto ..." The star glanced at the dancer floating above.

Siona followed the star's gaze. She flicked her tail and rose up to where the dancer fluttered in shades of red, orange, and yellow. Siona swallowed. "I'd like to ask you something," said Siona to the dancer, "and it's okay if you say no because ... because ..."

"No, no," cried Clarissa. "Please, you must all stay here. Siona your life is … is …"

The trilobite turned to face the clam. Both antennae touched the damaged shell. Clarissa shook between the mother of pearl, wincing in pain.

"Your life is your life," said the trilobite to Siona. Looking back to the clam, he added, "We can sometimes know the past, and for some that see the future, there will be much jubilation when that vision blurs."

Siona turned back to the dancer and continued. "Because it could be dangerous. And I'm asking you to do something when I don't know what will happen next. But you have been there before. Out there, out in the open ocean with your own kind." Dancer fluttered in the water in silence. "Have you ever thought of going back to the open … sea …?" Siona's voice trailed off.

Dancer continued to float and flutter. The trilobite nodded to the creature, stepping back from the others. Dancer followed.

No one knows for sure what words passed between the two creatures. From the trilobite came a deep rumble that rode with the ebb and flow of the waves in the ocean. And to those words, Dancer danced. The trilobite paused, waiting for Dancer to reply. Dancer nodded. When they returned to the group, the trilobite spoke first.

"Dancer has agreed to take you to the portal. The portal is a mysterious place. We believe that the portal leads to the open ocean. Creatures such as Dancer have joined us through the portal. Creatures also have been lost. No creature that has entered the portal from our tide pool has ever returned." The trilobite paused and then asked, "Are you willing to risk your own lives to find him? The ocean is immense. Reilly is lost in that immensity."

Siona waited for the others to reply.

"I've got to use my rhinophores for something … special," said Harold.

"I've got to find out if I'm still the star that I was, even if I have only four arms," said Sydney.

"You'll always be a star to me," said the hare to Sydney.

"And you will always be special to me," said the star to the hare.

Siona looked at both. The star and the hare nodded in unison.

The dancer nodded as well, her frills unfolding, making ready for the journey.

There was a flash of red. The bright, young red ragworm paddled into the midst of the group. "I am going with you!" she cried, and all eyes turned to her. "I … I … I …" she stammered, "have really strong fangs. You might need an extra set of fangs. An extra set of fangs might come in handy!"

"That is a wonderful offer," said Siona, "but I would not feel right about that. It's too risky, and I think Reilly would feel awful if something happened to you."

The red worm faced Siona. She spread her paddles wide and laughed until she cried. "Risk? Risk? All living things live in peril!" she cried. "These pools are filled with danger; every day we face humongous odds, sea spiders, and nasty pistol shrimp. When we talk about risk, all we consider are the chances that something bad might happen. But risk also implies that there is a chance something good—something *wonderful*—can happen. We can even calculate that." And she used her adroit fangs to draw the mathematical equation of the chances that a good thing would happen:

$$pGood = 1 - pBad$$

The red worm pointed with her fangs to the equation written in the sand. "See, pGood is the probability, or chance, that we will find Reilly, rescue him, and bring him to safety. And pBad is the probability of not finding Reilly and not … and not …" The young red worm hesitated, unable to complete the sentence.

"That equation seems pretty straightforward to me," interrupted Harold. "And she does have a very nice set of fangs. They could be really helpful."

Sydney nodded. "I think Reilly would appreciate a lovely set of fangs."

"Oh, and you can call me Kate," said the young red worm.

"And don't forget about me!" called Bernie, getting their attention with the sweep of his tail. "I'm coming with you too. My nanoscale whiskers and cellulose blend might be exactly what Reilly needs." Using his tail as a pointer, Bernie showed them the orange nanoscale whiskers on the tip of his head between his eyes.

"But Bernie, it will be too dangerous," cried Siona.

Bernie laughed and swum to her side. "Danger is being an orange-marked squirt among the pure white. My kind is unwelcome here. I'm going with you."

The portal was located at the end of a long, twisting tributary that branched from the main basin of the tide pool just beyond the rock fortress that had protected the young sea squirts from the pistol shrimp's assault. As the animals approached the portal, the tributary narrowed. The rock walls on either side grew higher as the water's depth increased, forming a narrow canyon. The light of the dwindling day diminished. Only sparse clumps of algae grew. As the animals approached, the algae bent and trembled in the jetting water. Against this current, the animals braced themselves as they neared the portal. The portal looked very much like a lava tube, but it was completely smooth as if it had been hollowed out by precision tools and skilled hands. Water from the incoming tide would fill the portal. As it filled, water would flow out of the portal into the tide pool. When the portal filled, it would become a temporary siphon, and the torrent of water would reverse course, hastening through the portal and back to the sea.

Dancer hovered over the animals. She motioned them close and dropped down to the sandy bottom. They climbed aboard her waving body. Sydney, now in control of his hydraulics, held firmly to Dancer with two of his arms. With the other two he held Harold tight. Kate worked her way under one of Sydney's strong arms and clutched one side of Harold. Once the larger animals were aboard, Dancer covered them with her carpet-like body, forming a roll. Into this roll both Siona and Bernie swam, rolling up into the lacy gills of the dancer, creating tiny rolls within a roll. The trilobite pushed the multianimal roll into position between an outcropping of rock and the mouth of the portal.

The right side of Clarissa's shell flapped in the torrent of the water. With the shell unhinged, the crack had grown to a gap. "Godspeed, Siona! Godspeed all," cried the clam.

"Thank you, Clarissa. Thank you so much for everything," replied Siona, her voice muffled. "We will see you again soon!"

Clarissa cried again, unhinged.

Rolled up like a sushi roll, Siona and the others could feel the rush of water spilling in from the portal, pushing them back against the rock outcropping. If the rocks had not been there, they would have been pushed back into the tide pool. As the portal filled with water, it turned into a temporary siphon, and the forces reversed. The animals were not prepared for the rush of water that sucked them into the portal. They were swept into the chute like a bobsledding team from the tropics. Dancer held them tight in the carpet of her body as they torpedoed down the lava tube. They had no driver, no brakeman. The tube first rolled to the left and then to the right, then left, another left, a sharp right, and then a long straightaway, in which they were going so fast that they felt as if their epidermises would surely separate from their dermises. Down the long straightaway they raced. They were so wrapped up in Dancer's parapodia that no one could see the light at the end of the tunnel growing bigger and brighter. Out of the chute they shot, plummeting up through the water. They breached the surface of the water like a submarine emerging from the depths after an emergency blow. They sailed through the air, and with their airborne arch completed, they splashed down into the comfort of the sea.

Harold opened his mouth to speak. All he could say was something that sounded a bit like, "A at tha re ly an totly scar y. I s o gad we l be he re."

Still rolled up in the threadlike gills of the dancer, Bernie cried, "Yee-haw!" He wiped his tail over his eyes. "That was the greatest ride of my entire life! Man, I wasn't sure that we would make it. That right-hand turn was totally insane!" Bernie thumped his tail. "And we go that way!" he said, pointing with his tail. "We follow the flow of the tide. That way we can catch up to Reilly."

Siona shared Bernie's enthusiasm and sense of direction, as squirts together are apt to do. She wiggled free from the lacy gills and swam from Dancer's back. She beat her tail, and into the gray she went. Light gray above, dark gray below disappearing into black. Down and down and up and up and from side to side, there was nothing but the sea.

The sandy bottom of the tide pool was gone. The rocks were gone. The algae anchored in the sand were gone. Siona had known that the ocean was a big place, but this space—the size of it, the above, the below, the gray on all sides—reached to touch infinity. And somewhere in all this gray, Siona knew that a brilliant yellow ragworm labored, wounded and alone. Her tail drooped. *How will we ever find Reilly? Is it possible? Can impossible things happen?* Siona felt the pressure of the sea above, its heavy weight. She emitted two tiny sighs to relieve the pressure she felt inside.

But the pressure building up in the tiny squirt was not alone. Below, the seafloor pressure was growing. Hot magma was on the rise. The temperature of the magma was over 1,200 degrees Celsius. That is very, very hot. The seafloor rumbled. From the depths, gas and heat struggled for freedom. The earth was restless. And so was Siona. She swam alongside the dancer and glanced at the others. She caught Sydney's gaze, and the star, looking very pleased with himself, pointed a single tube foot straight up from the tip of one of his arms (such was his newfound control of his hydraulics), giving Siona a thumps-up. Kate slipped out from under the star's arms to swim alongside Siona. Her bright red paddles moved easily through the gray. The red worm smiled, her fangs arching perfectly. Harold, secure under the strong arms of the star, waved his rhinophores in circles, searching for Reilly's scent. He glanced at Siona and gave her a wink. Bernie wiggled free of the dancer's lacy gills to swim with Siona and Kate. The dancer unfurled her frills to their greatest extent, flapping and following the long slow pull of the tide.

"Do we keep going this way?" asked the bright red ragworm, clicking her fangs together.

"Of course we do!" cried Bernie. "We go the way we are going." He swept his long tail through the water.

Siona sighed. She swam with small short strokes that took her back to Dancer. She rolled herself into the lacy gills and sighed again. *Oh, Reilly, we're trying. We are trying ... trying? Does that even count?* Siona pretended to study the delicate gills that held her tight. She glanced up at the others around her. *Trying does not mean a thing.* One was either successful, or one failed. If her inkling was right, Reilly's grandfather's-great-great-grandfather's father had once sought to cut the claw of a pistol shrimp, and he had failed. It was not the attempt of the deed but only its failure that was recorded and passed down, generation to generation. And here she was with her friends, who had followed her into deep water. She sighed again and, for a moment, sank her head into the squishy body of the hare. The moment was short, and Siona focused with apparently keen interest again on the lacy gills of Dancer. But it was too late. Harold, through constrained by the arms of the star, twisted to take a look at the squirt. Siona tried to smile but only grimaced. The hare nodded, his rhinophores straight and true, his eyes clear and bright.

"Let me reassure you," said the hare to no one in particular. "With these babies"—he swung his rhinophores from right to left—"we can find Reilly. Our mission may be improbable, but it is not impossible!" He sang out to the sea ahead and to his companions. There was a pause. Even Dancer held her body still.

Siona gave a little cough. "Harold, would you mind repeating that ... that last bit?"

"Certainly," said the hare. And this time, he opened up the deep, rich vibrato of his sea hare voice and sang mightily into the mighty ocean. "Our mission is *im-prob-able* but most *cer-tain-ly not im-poss-i-ble*."

By now we all know how fast and far sound travels in water. The waves of sound flooded the waves of water.

Far away, floating on the surface of the water, a once-brilliant-yellow ragworm stirred, his breathing labored. He dreamed of a sea hare singing a song. It was a beautiful song of hope. A bright red ragworm sailed through an inside-out, upside-down circle, ending at his side, her fangs arching perfectly. A tiny squirt called his name.

"See?" said the squirt with a flip of her long tail. "See? What could not be done is done."

The worm rose high on the surface of a wave. He rose so high that he touched the wispy clouds hanging in the sky. Below, the ocean gleamed turquoise and silver. A bright orb above cut a path of gold on the swelling sea. Down went the wave and the worm. In the trough of the wave, walls of gray rose high above the pale yellow worm.

In the distance, Siona heard a rumble. Beneath her, she felt Dancer tremble. The dancer shook; her frills turned dark red.

"Hey," Siona called to Bernie and Kate from the dancer's back. "I think Dancer wants you to come back."

Dancer dipped under Bernie and the bright red ragworm, lifting them up. Kate slid back under one of Sydney's arms. Bernie rolled up in the lacy gills, right next to Siona. Sydney increased his grip on the hare. The rumble grew into a roar. Dancer fluttered and flapped; she raced, ascending through the sea, carrying her cargo up as the gray turned many shades lighter. When she had nearly reached the surface, she came to a stop, resting on the waves. Siona wiggled free and swam a few tentative strokes from the dancer. Below, colossal shadows voyaged from the darkness. There were at least a dozen creatures, the ancestors of *Anomalocaris canadensis*, so large they were like cargo ships and Siona a lonely kayaker. The lobed eyes of the creatures below swept from right to left, their large, curling, netlike appendages forcing diatoms and rotifers into cavernous mouths. Siona hovered alongside Dancer until the monsterous creatures became dark shadows again, disppearing as they journeyed past.

A warm wind whispered across the water, making waves. Up and down, the creatures rose and fell. Bernie called out to Siona, and she turned to face him. High on the wave, mere microns below the surface of the water, Siona saw the bright orange orb burning on the lip of the horizon. Bernie was a dark silhouette as he approached. Siona pointed at the orb with her tail. Alongside Siona, Bernie turned to face the burning ball.

"It's so beautiful," said Bernie. "I bet no other squirt has ever seen such a sight."

"And maybe," said Siona, "no squirt should."

She turned away from Bernie to inspect the tip of her tail so he would not see her cry. She heard Bernie murmur, and she looked back. The view held her tail still. The burning orb cast colors across the deepening sapphire blue of the ocean. Wisps of clouds turned a luminous scarlet. *But what of the others?* thought Siona. She glanced back at her motley group of friends. Carried on Dancer's back, they, too, stared at the bright orb hovering at the edge of the open ocean. Siona had led them here, to the open ocean, to the devastatingly beautiful view of a great bright orb dropping in the sky. The orb slipped below the edge of the horizon. In the final heartbeats of the day, the sky bled crimson. The colors faded. The clouds turned gray. The shimmering lights on the ocean waves vanished. It grew dark. The sea and sky turned black. Siona floated just below the surface, a tiny miniscule being in a dark abyss. With rueful recognition, Siona hung her head, her long tail listless. She was cold and without a rock in sight. All she could do now was to keep on swimming.

In the darkness, she heard Harold. "My, it's gloomy out here. I guess no one happened to see any red algae anywhere." There was a tremor in his voice. "Something seems to be wrong with Dancer. She is not moving very much," he added.

"It's okay," said Sydney, still holding him tight. "Dancer is sleeping. This is what happens to dancers at night. They stop dancing."

"It would be nice to have some light out here," said the hare. "I think maybe we should head back to the tide pool, and we can start searching again tomorrow in the light." He compressed his squishy body into the quiet body of the dancer. "Oh, no!" cried Harold. "Stay away, Siona and Bernie! Stay away. I am so sorry!"

In the darkness, Siona and Bernie could not see that the hare had released a cloud of ink.

"I think I might be scared or something," said Harold in apology.

"Oh heck, Harold," cried Sydney, holding on to the hare and doing his best to keep his tube feet under control, as the unseen cloud of ink rose from the very creature the star aimed to protect.

With a quick flick of her tail, Siona pushed Bernie away from the cloud of noxious ink, and they swam away to a safe distance.

"I'm sorry! I'm sorry!" cried the hare. "It's so black and rockless here. I want to go home! I want to go home!"

The wind moved across the water. Only a thin veil of the sea covered the creatures. In the moonless night, thousands upon thousands of blinking little lights sprung up across the night sky, bright flowers in a black meadow.

"Look!" Siona called. "Look up, Harold. Look up!"

Harold looked up. "Oh, thank you tiny lights!" cried the hare. "Oh, you are so lovely. Can you hear me? Can you come a bit closer? I'm right here. Will you come beside me and share your light with me?"

Siona tried calling to the stars. "Hey, you bright things! Look down here. Here we are, right here. See us? Please—we beg you to come closer!"

The stars held their ground, unmoved by Siona's pleas. Light, for which the hare was so grateful, erupted from that cluster of stars, traveling at the ludicrous speed of 670 million miles per hour, taking more than four years to reach the terrified eyes of the hare. In the light of the stars, the creatures unknowingly caught a glimpse of the past, spellbound and star-struck in a hopelessly clear dark night. The closest star, twinkling with a red hue, held its position more than 24,984,000,000,000 miles away. Later, the primates with the big brains would call that star Proxima Centauri.

Around that star a small exoplanet whirled, completing an orbit every 11.2 earth days, its sky a burnt yellow-orange. There, too, water sloshed, froze, and steamed, a rarity in the universe. The creatures on that planet with their big brains gazed into the starry night sky. They wondered how they might reach out through space to say hello to those on the blue ball of a planet that we now call Earth, though they had a different name for it. But before the light from the tiny star reached Siona and her friends, the orange-colored, bulbous leader of the exoplanet crept out of his golden tower, with trumpetlike instruments blaring. The creatures there with their big brains polluted their planet, filled it with toxins, and fought and argued and warred so much that life on that far planet came to a near end. Only microbial mats were left to start the process all over again.

The ink of the hare had dissipated. Siona flipped her tail in the water, setting out to return to the lacy gills of the dancer. Bernie swam at her side. Bright blue lights exploded around the squirts. Bernie came to a quick stop. Siona gasped and thrust herself forward to escape the flash of light. As Siona fled, more lights erupted, creating a ribbon of bright blue across the black water.

"Cool," said Bernie.

Siona slowed and came to a stop. The blue light vanished, and darkness returned. She gave her tail a tiny swish, and the bright blue lights appeared again. Siona remained still and the lights disappeared. She swam a small circle in the water, and a ring of bright blue emerged. She swam a figure eight, and a blue figure eight floated on the water.

"Cool," said Bernie again.

"Wonderful!" cried Harold. "The little lights from the sky have joined us!"

Siona wiggled her tail and peered intently at the bright blue lights. Riding in the water, she saw scores of glowing wee sea beasties. They were like tiny fireflies of the sea. *Bam, bam, bam* went Siona's tail in the water, creating tiny bubbles, turning the water turbulent, jostling the tiny creatures. Inside the creatures, the special enzyme widget luciferase turned on as if a light switch had been flipped. It was named after Lucifer, before the fall from grace—the shining one, the light-bearer. But how could that happen? How could a bunch of bubbles and swirling water change a protein, or enzyme widget, deep inside a cell? (Have you ever wondered why you can feel it when someone pokes you in the arm?)

The bubbles bombarded the tiny creatures, activating mechanoreceptors linked to wee channel widgets that opened their doors to the sodium salt ions in the sea. In rushed the sodium and a wave of electricity propagated through the cytosol of the single-celled creatures. In response, calcium ions rushed out of their little reservoirs, crossing the cytosol to bind to the surface of a large vacuole, opening calcium-dependent, voltage-gated proton (H^+) channels. With the channels open, the protons spilled out of the vacuole, acidifying the adjacent scintillon organelle, the home of the enzyme widget luciferase. The protons, the hydrogen ions, the most abundant and tiniest elements in the universe, with their electrons lost, flipped the switch, turning on luciferase—and there was light; a billion photons flashed to snatch away the darkness.

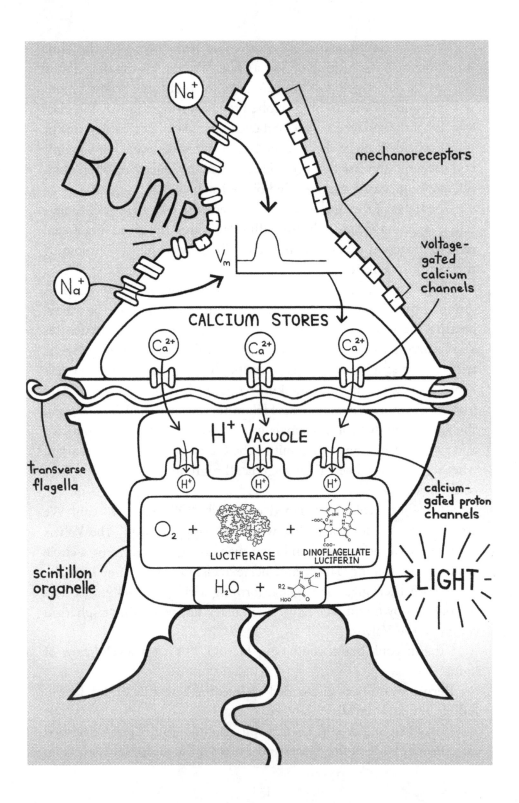

When Siona listened closely, she could hear them sing the same little tune with the beating of Siona's tail. "We are the dinoflagellates! We are the dinoflagellates! We can make the nighttime bright!" Siona was reminded of the flashing strobe lights coursing through the glass spicules of the sponge that she had encountered earlier that day. So the stars in the dark night sky and the bright sun at day were not the only entities in the universe that could lay claim to the generation of photons. So, too, could small, single-celled biological beings.

The lights of the tiny creatures erupted with every swish of Siona's tail. Caught in the blue light from dinoflagellates, the green fluorescent protein widgets in a nearby family of jellyfish glowed green, illuminating their cathedral-like caps.

Siona beat her tail until she grew tired. She needed to sleep. A group of spherical Cambrian Volvox colonies rolled past in the waves, beating the water with massive flagella—those whiplike structures a reoccurring theme in biological systems. Every beat of the flagella triggered the flight of photons from the dinoflagellates. From Siona's experience in the sponge, she knew a great deal about flagella. And from her early conversation with Helamite, the nocturnal *Hallucigenia*, she also knew that some animals were active at night. Siona put two and two together. She called out to the Cambrian colonies and asked whether they could beat their flagella all night long, and, if so, if they could help.

The Volvox colonies laughed out loud. "Of course we can! We are nocturnal," they cried. "We would be happy to help!" The Volvox gathered with their cousins and their many daughters, forming a circle around the sleeping dancer and her exhausted cargo. They beat the water with their gigantic flagella, forming a ring of black polka dots surrounded by bright blue light. Each black dot was a single spherical colony of the Volvox.

"Thank you! Thank you!" sang Harold. "What a lovely show of lights!"

Bernie swam back and curled up into the lacy gills of the dancer, falling into an immediate slumber.

Harold sighed deeply, his rhinophores drooping. The hare nestled into the soft body of the dancer and drifted off to sleep, softly singing,

"Little lights, little lights." Siona swam to the dancer and rolled herself up in the lacy gills next to Bernie. With the aid of the Volvox, dinoflagellates, jellies, and the stars above, Siona and her friends found their own personal night-lights.

9

Bubbles and Fangs to the Rescue

THE BLACKNESS RECEDED, AND A pale yellow crack of light chiseled between the gray sea and sky. Siona woke and, with a few strokes of her tail, swam out into the open ocean. She could no longer see the wee lights of the dinoflagellates, and their songs had subsided. As the earth twirled on its axis, spinning at one thousand miles an hour, the bright orange orb rose, casting a pale yellow ribbon across the steely gray of the sea. Siona turned to look back at the others. Dancer still slept; her winglike parapodia fluttered. Sydney held tight to the hare. Kate rested under one of the star's strong arms. Bernie's tail wiggled, still rolled up tight in the lacy gills. Harold slept with a beautific smile on his face. They were adrift. Only the dancer was at home out in the open sea.

Siona hung her head. *What have I done? All because I wanted to keep my tail. Reilly would not have ever wanted us to follow him here. What if …?* "I am so sorry," she said to her sleeping companions.

The yellow crack in the sky widened. As the sea turned from gray to blue, her apology was ignored.

Miles away, the seafloor rumbled under the deep ocean. Scorching-hot orange lava oozed through cracks. Chilled by cold water, the lava morphed to black stone. Chimneys rose from the ocean floor like the skyscrapers of some alien metropolis. They belched black boiling water. Hydrogen sulfide. Minerals and gunk. It reeked of sulfur. Except for the occasional glow of molten lava and the flash of light from bioluminescent sponges, it was dark. Not a ray of sunshine reached the depths of the belching chimneys.

In the absence of the sunlight, life had found a way. Chemolithotrophic microbes harnessed energy and fuel from the reeking molecules and elements of the dead. An entire food web flourished, not from sunshine but from the heat and chemicals churning from the earth. Archaea and bacteria lined the chimneys and valleys, creating a microbial pasture upon which other animals grazed. Single-celled amoebas, with their pseudopodia extended like little arms, engulfed microbes. A velvety sulfide worm used his tiny proboscis to spoon up amoebas and microbes. A blind ghost shrimp used her claw as a fork, dining on the worms. Giant clams opened their shells, filtering the sea. Blind Lobsterish Ones stalked the ghost shrimp. Brittle stars hunted clams. Giant tube worms towered between the chimneys, anchored at their ends in the rich bed of goo and decay.

As Siona and her companions drifted in the open ocean, the chimneys spewed more than the usual amount of hot, black, sulfurous water. The velvety sulfide worms sensed the impending doom and crept away from the towering chimneys.

It was time for the others to wake up. Siona nudged the dancer, whose frills fluttered. Siona tapped one of Sydney's arms with her tail. His tube feet pumped. She bounced the hare's rhinophores, wiggled one of Kate's paddles, and tickled Bernie with her tail. Siona pointed in the direction they should take, away from the rising sun. Harold woke and swept his rhinophores in a slow circle, searching for a scent. He shook his head. The dancer unfurled her parapodia as far as she could. Off they went, heading away from the sun.

Kate slid off Dancer and pushed from behind to add some extra propulsion. Riding in the lacy gills, Siona smiled at Kate. The young red worm picked up the tempo. Perhaps she would not have paddled quite so hard had she known that each stroke of her paddles took them deeper out into the ocean, away from the very place that they needed to be in order to survive—away from the rocky shores and tide pools of the geologically fleeting supercontinent that would later give birth to places called South America, Africa, Arabia, Madagascar, India,

Australia, and Antarctica. It was so large, this super gigantic continent, that it was hard to imagine that Siona and her friends had no clue where it might be found.

They were likely under too much pressure in their search for the worm. Beneath the ocean, great plates in the crust and solid mantle of the earth were also under pressure. The ocean floor burped, and gas escaped. A large bubble lifted from the seafloor.

The great bubble rose—up, up it went. The bubble struck Dancer's left side, knocking her upside down. Sydney found himself holding on to the upside-down Dancer with three arms. One arm clung to the hare. The hare began to slide. The tube feet on the arm slipped with the weight of the hare until only two tube feet held a single rhinophore. The tube feet stretched; the rhinophore stretched. And then, with a *pop*, the tube feet contracted, losing their hold on the hare. Harold did not have time to call out; he simply sank, his rhinophores going every which way. Recovering, Dancer flapped, plunging after the hare. Kate paddled in pursuit of the hare, in the dancer's wake. Bernie and Siona rode the wild ride down, tangled in the lacy gills. Sydney held on by his feet.

As Harold twisted in the water, he began to shout. "Zinc! Zinc!" cried the Hare, sinking in the water. "I caught his scent! Reilly's scent!" His rhinophores pointed northwest as he twirled in the water, like the eyes of a ballerina focused on one spot as she pirouettes faster and faster. As he spun, his rhinophores swished through the water to point down the path of scent molecules.

The dancer maneuvered to avoid a slew of rising bubbles, like a spaceship avoiding meteorites. As they descended, the water grew darker and dense. With the darkness came the pressure. Kate had trouble breathing. She was at her depth limit. The pressure of the ocean above weighed heavily. The young red worm began to gasp; her paddling became chaotic and out of control. Dancer, in a last-ditch effort, dipped under the worm. Sydney reached out with two of his arms and seized the nearly unconscious worm, pulling her onto Dancer's back.

"We have to go up!" screamed the star. "Kate cannot survive at this depth!"

Like a defeated search-and-rescue party descending Mount Everest, the dancer ascended in the water. As they rose, the young red worm stirred.

"I'm okay," Kate said finally. Dancer came to a stop, hovering in the water. Kate peered over the parapodia, down into the darkness. "I am so sorry, Harold. I am so sorry."

Siona wiggled free from the lacy gills. "The depth won't bother me. I'm too little; I'll be back. I'm going to get—"

At that moment a big bubble bumped into Siona and continued on its way, catching her in its buoyancy. Up it went without any regard to its passenger. Siona struggled to escape the bubble. She heard a sharp crack as the bubble beneath her burst. She tumbled for a moment before regaining control. Below her, Kate looked up; her sharp fangs opened and closed. She smiled with her fangs arching perfectly.

"What a way to burst someone's bubble!" cried Bernie, looking at Kate, who had recovered remarkably well.

More bubbles passed on their voyage up. Siona watched their ascension.

"I have an idea!" she cried. "Stay here, all of you. I will be back soon with Harold."

And she dove, plunging with her head down, her muscles and widgets strained. She darted right and left to avoid the hail of bubbles. "I need more power!" she squeaked in the depth. "Come on, you widgets! Give me more power!" Her tail thrashed with might. Her widgets responded and gathered fatty acids, long chains of carbon molecules, fuel held in reserve. The widgets fed those fatty acids to the biological engines, the mitochondria, of her cells, like firemen adding coal to the boiler of a steam train. But that engine required oxygen. And when the oxygen levels declined in the depths, Siona's widgets switched to another engine running in her cells—the glycolytic engine, burning sugar reserves with the spinning of eleven little turbines in the cytosol of her cells. That gave her the power she needed as she descended into twilight.

"Sing, sing, Harold!" Siona squeaked in the darkness. "I can't see you!"

Below her and to the right, Siona heard the hare squeak out a song. Carried in the water, the song triggered the activation of bioluminescent bacteria, nestled in sweet symbiosis with their sponges. Light from the microbes traveled through the glass spicules of the sponges as if through well-engineered optical fibers, the fibers thinner than a human hair. On the seafloor, a beacon of light wavered.

"Sing louder," squeaked Siona, recalling her experience when she was stuck in the sponge, with the lights flashing in response to the sea squirt songs.

The hare sang loudly. Below him, the lights turned on. Siona saw the silhouette of the hare.

"Harold!" Siona squeaked. "I'm right here! Just above you."

The hare looked up, his body squished under the pressure. One rhinophore pointed northwest and the other pointed right at Siona.

"Siona!" squeaked the hare. "What are you doing down here?"

"I'm going to get you a bubble," Siona squeaked.

"A bubble?"

Siona dove below the hare in pursuit of a titanic bubble rising from the depths to his left. She reached the bubble, and, in the light of the sponges, gave the bubble a push, like a little tugboat pushing a barge into port. The bubble yielded and rose up directly under the hare. With the bubble's course corrected, Siona swam to the top of the bubble. Up rose the great bubble, and, catching Harold, it continued on its journey, carrying a cargo of two. As the bubble spun, Harold kept one rhinophore pointing northwest, the other at Siona. Rising together, Harold smiled at Siona, and Siona smiled at him. He winked and sang, his voice no longer a squeak but deep and rich.

> It's you that I shall ever adore
> With each and every rhinophore.
> You smell so sweet,
> It is such a treat!
> Your sweetness will forever more
> Go down in the history of animal lore.

Dancer, Kate, Bernie, and Sydney heard the song of the hare before they saw him. They knew how fast sound traveled in water. Dancer held very still. Kate, peering down from Dancer's back, was the first to see. She readied her fangs. From the depths, the bubble with the precious cargo rose up above the dancer. Bernie cried out in glee, and Sydney waved one arm with near hysterics. As the bubble rose, Dancer positioned herself right below. Kate streaked up, her fangs opened wide. There was a piercing crack as her fangs snapped shut. The bubble exploded. Down tumbled the hare. Dancer corrected her position. Sydney rose up on one arm; the other three spread like a catcher's glove. As the hare fell, he made contact with one of the three arms. The suctions on each tube foot hit their maximum, and the other two arms of the star grabbed the hare, pulling Harold aboard the fluttering raft of the dancer's back. It wasn't so much that the star held the hare as that the star hugged the hare. Bernie again cried out in glee, and Kate clicked her fangs.

Siona hovered above, watching the scene below. "Great job, Siona!"

they cried. She swam to join her friends. She smiled weakly and rolled herself up in the lacy gills, pressing into the soft back of the dancer so no one could see her cry. She had helped to save the hare, but who would or could save them all? *It's my fault.* She pressed harder into the soft back. *All because I wanted to keep my tail!*

"Sydney, your feet are smashing my rhinophores!"

"I am so sorry; I guess even my feet are so happy to see you!"

The hare beamed. "I'm so happy to see you too! We have to go while the scent is strong. I have the scent of zinc and courage! My rhinophores are locked on. Dancer, go left. Full speed ahead!"

Dancer turned to the left.

"Yes, a bit more rightish now."

Again, Dancer corrected her flight in the water.

"A bit more left now, just a wee tad."

Dancer corrected her course again.

"The scent is getting fainter; we need more speed. Dancer, can you go faster?"

Kate slid off the back and paddled, pushing from behind. Dancer was flying through the water, propelled by the paddling worm and her own fluttering body. Sydney held Harold tight. Harold, with his rhinophores sticking straight out, learned to lean his weight one way or another to control their headlong flight down a path of molecules, present in the sea in only one part per billion. Bernie cried out, encouraging them all. Siona shook her head. She blinked her eyes to stop the tears as she looked from the dancer to Kate, from Bernie to the star and hare. They were all far from the protection of the tide pools; they were focused on a single goal, buoyed by hope and a fluttering dancer. Like a honking horn, Harold sang out into the sea, calling for Reilly, knowing how fast and far sound travels in water.

And from faraway, a pale yellow worm, floating in the waves, dreamed of the sea hare's song. He dreamed of a time long ago—1.78 billion years earlier—when oceanic cyanobacteria bloomed, and rich microbial mats grew thick. In his dream, he saw the cyanobacteria capture light from the sun for energy as they spewed out a toxic gas. The microbial mats, like wee chemical plants, contributed to the pollution.

Small microbes changed the climate. It was the Great Oxidation Event. Like a toxic cloud, the gas sickened and killed scores of anaerobic creatures and turned the planet cold and icy, like a giant snowball. Only those creatures that could adapt survived the cold and the toxic gas—oxygen.

Millions and millions of years later, the primates with the big brains chopped down the trees across entire continents. Each tree was a carbon dioxide (CO_2) sink by virtue of the enzyme widget RuBisCo. The carbon captured created sugars for the trees from sunshine. The primates with the big brains built factories and cars, churning out more CO_2. And like the blue-green algae they, too, changed the climate. The oceans acidified. Corals bleached. Diatoms lost their silica shells and sank to the sludge below. Billions of oyster larvae died, their enzyme widgets unable to make shells in the corrosive new chemistry of the seas. The primates with the big brains pulled in their profits, until there was nothing more to gain. At the edge of the sea, the primates with the big brains shivered in the heat.

Reilly shivered in the water. His energy waned, but in his dream it continued. Wee microbes adapted after the Great Oxidation Event, altering their widgets with time. With the new widgets, the microbes harnessed oxygen to make energy, something Reilly so desperately needed now. Inside the microbes, biochemical turbines spun, spitting out electron donors with every cycle—three $NADH/H^+$ molecules here and one $FADH_2$ there. The electrons from those molecules entered a chain of membrane-bound widgets. From one widget to the next, the electrons bumped down this electron transport chain, powering the pumping of tiny protons or charged hydrogen atoms, from one side of a membrane to the other, driving an electrochemical gradient, creating a biological battery.

The protons fled screaming down the electrochemical gradient through tiny ATP synthase widgets, anchored like tunnels in the membrane. The flow of protons triggered a little twist in the ATP synthase widget, generating ATP—the biological currency of energy. And that's what Reilly needed. He needed energy.

He took one more breath. One of his five hearts squeezed. He dreamed of the tiny microbe, with its clever electron transport chain and biochemical turbines. In his dream, the tiny microbe, by sheer chance, bumped into a larger microbe and was accidentally engulfed. After that, for more than a billion years, the two were inseparable—the bigger microbe and little one that had learned to use oxygen to generate energy. Each microbe benefited from the other, growing together and multiplying as one. Over time, the smaller microbes lost their autonomy and became subservient organelles—the mitochondria. The mitochondria became little engines, or power plants, in cells of eukaryotic creatures, such as Reilly the Ragworm.

With Reilly's last breath, another engine labored. It was harbored in the cytosol and slop of his cells. The smaller glycolytic engine whirled, its eleven widget turbines spinning, desperate to power brain cells and muscles and beating hearts. But this little engine could not. The turbines whirled to a stop. There was no more energy to power the worm. He floated, drifting in the water, his biological batteries spent.

The sun had already reached its apex for the day and was on its journey west. Dancer flapped her frills. A small tear ran through the yellow border of the back flap of her left parapodium. Kate paddled, pushing Dancer from behind to help keep their course true. Kate's seventh paddle on the right barely moved. Sydney had lost turgor pressure in twenty-six of his tube feet. The limp feet jiggled in unison with the flapping of Dancer's parapodia. Bernie and Siona swam alongside Dancer to reduce the load, if only by a small degree.

"Wait! Wait!" cried Harold. "I think I've detected an increase in the concentration gradient! The scent is stronger!" The hare leaned to the right. "Go there, Dancer! There! I think we are getting close!"

The others picked up the pace, bobbing along in the gray water. Siona, taking the angle and direction of the hare's rhinophores, swam ahead. Shadows from the waves above generated lopsided circles in the wind. Ahead, Siona saw nothing but gray water. Only the hare could see the ragworm's path ahead, dusted with molecules of zinc and mettle and grit, with his sense of scent.

"Oh!" cried Harold. He leaned very hard to the right, and Dancer nearly reversed course. Siona stopped in the water. She turned to the right as well. Ahead was a blur, an indistinct pale shadow floating above in waves. "Oh!" cried Harold again. Siona beat her tail. They all aimed for that blur. The blur turned a pale yellow. Siona heard Kate gasp and cry out. As they approached, the blur grew paddles, defined by twenty segments. A set of fine, strong fangs hung limp from a drooping head. A tiny shaft of sunlight pierced the gaping hole between the worm's sixth and seventh segments, where the bayonet from the shrimp had run its course.

Dancer carried the star alongside the worm. A single strong arm of the star reached out with tube feet stretched, the turgor pressure restored. They caught their target—the pale yellow worm—pulling him on board the dancer.

"Now! Now!" cried the star to Bernie and Siona. "Use your nanoscale whiskers and cellulose blend!"

Siona and Bernie went to work, Bernie on the dorsal side and Siona at the ventral, where the wound was wider. Together they filled the hole with their nanoscale whiskers. Siona looked at Bernie. She swam to the top of the worm. She could see the orange nanoscale whiskers covered the wound. She swam back to the underside of the worm. There, her blue nanoscale whiskers filled the hole on the other side.

"What's happening?" asked Harold. "Why doesn't Reilly wake up?" Kate cried.

"I don't know," whispered Bernie and Siona together.

"It might take some time," said Sydney. "It took time for the tear in my arm to heal." The star held the worm at the middle. The ends of the worm floated.

They drifted in the water. The sun fell to the west. Caught on the lip of the horizon, the sun sent silent rays of scarlet and orange across the sea and disappeared. The sea turned black, the sky a deep navy. And they waited. The stars bloomed. The dinoflagellates sang. There were no colonial Volvox, so Siona, Bernie, and Kate took turns making blue ribbons flash bright to comfort Harold and themselves. With the flash of blue light from the dinoflagellates, entire families of jellies fluoresced green as they paraded past. Siona and the others waited. The earth spun. Dawn loomed gray, then pale yellow, as pale as a quiet ragworm. The sun rose. Light stuck gleaming fangs. And they waited. Siona and Bernie inspected the nanoscale whiskers. They mumbled that the whiskers seemed to work. The gaping hole was gone.

"Maybe we were too late," whispered Sydney. Too many tube feet went slack from sorrow. The pale yellow worm slipped from under the star's arm and floated free. In grief, Kate rubbed her front paddles against her fangs; she rubbed them together hard. She looked at the vacant spot beside her, where the yellow worm had been. She dropped her fangs to Dancer's back. The spark from her fangs shot like a bolt of lightning. Dancer fluttered madly. Harold trembled, his rhinophores upright and rigid. Sydney lost control of three of his arms, holding Harold to the fibrillating body of the dancer with half an arm. Both Bernie and Siona were blasted from the lacy gills, and Kate herself was left blinking behind them all.

"*Oh!*" cried Harold, recovering. "That shock must have been from the metal in your fangs, Kate."

Siona looked from Kate's fangs to the drooping fangs of the yellow worm. "That's it!" she cried. "Kate, you can transfer your mettle to Reilly! Rub your paddles against your fangs, and then touch Reilly's fangs with yours. Maybe we can turn him back on."

Kate rubbed her paddles against her fangs as hard and as fast as she could, and she approached the floating, pale yellow worm. "Clear! All clear!" she screamed. Her fangs touched Reilly's. He twitched. Kate rubbed her paddles and fangs together again. "Come on, Reilly. Come back. Come back!" She touched him again, and he twitched, his paddles moving in all directions. "Reilly, please," begged Kate, crying. Siona, with tears in her eyes, swam to the worms. She touched Reilly's wounds, adding more nanoscale whiskers. Reilly rolled in the water and coughed. He coughed again.

"He's waking up! He's waking up!" cried Siona.

Dancer flew to Reilly's side. Sydney leaned way over and grabbed the yellow worm. Harold sang into the sea.

Reilly blinked and opened his eyes. He saw Siona and smiled. Kate hovered above Reilly, her fangs arching perfectly. Reilly gazed at Kate, his color returning. "I've never seen such a beautiful sight," Reilly whispered to the cheers and hoots of the others.

He was a brilliant yellow worm again. "You must all be crazy!" said

Reilly, after the cheering had died down. He gazed out across the open ocean. "I wish you hadn't been quite so crazy."

"Oh, we calculated the odds," said Harold. "We had it all figured out."

When Reilly asked how they planned on getting back to the tide pool, Bernie turned to look at the tip of his tail, and Sydney lifted one arm to test how well three of his tube feet could contract. Kate idly brushed one of her paddles against the dancer. Siona watched the hare's rhinophores orbit in slow circles, like scanning radars. Harold shook his head, unable to detect a single scent molecule from his beloved algae. The animals floated in deep water. However, with the events about to unfold, that water was not deep enough.

The ocean floor groaned. The burst of burning black water that billowed from the seafloor chimneys earlier was a small placeholder for what was to follow. Great plates under the ocean were on the move. Hundreds of miles away, one plate nonchalantly slipped under another plate. The sea floor rose, creating a new vertical rise. The deep sea chimneys swayed like skyscrapers in an earthquake. The tallest of those careened to the ocean floor, to the chagrin of the creatures that lived in the valley below. A young, pale-white Lobsterish One was nearly crushed by a falling chimney. As luck would have it, the creature scurried and was saved by a crack.

A tsunami wave formed. In the very deep ocean, the ensuing wave was hardly noticeable, not much more than a bump in the water. But as the seafloor rose on its approach to land, so too did the wave, until it became a wall of water. Stirred by the winds, a rogue wave rose to join the tsunami. The combined wave headed for Siona and her friends at five hundred miles per hour.

Siona was the first to see the wall of water surging right for them.

"Quick! Everyone under Sydney's arms! Dancer, roll up as tight as you can!" cried Siona.

Sydney lifted three of his arms, and the others slid beneath them. Sydney slammed his arms down to secure his friends. The force of the suction of his tube feet made Dancer wince as she rolled her body around her companions. Siona swam into the lacy gills seconds before they were hit by the wave. The wall of water broke from above, slamming into the roll that was Dancer. Harold screamed. Sydney begged Harold not to squirt his ink. Kate begged Sydney to control his hydraulics.

"I don't want to die!" cried Harold. The water smacked them again, churning them with its watery claws.

"Hold on, everyone!" cried Siona.

"And I so much wanted to grow up," Bernie sobbed.

"Bernie, you will grow up, and I'll be there with you!" cried Siona.

Siona trembled in the lacy gills, holding her breath. She reached her tail over to Harold. "You can do this," she said to the hare. He looked at her with wild eyes, his rhinophores smashed under one of the star's arms, but he nodded.

"Hold with those feet of yours!" cried Siona to the star.

"I am. I can," cried Sydney, holding the others tight. "Even with only four arms!"

"And Dancer," whispered Siona into the lacy gills, "hold us. Hold us with all your might." And that's what the dancer did, her parapodia a dark blood red.

The will of the water shoved them to the tide pools lining the shore of the geologically fleeting giant continent. Rolling in the water, Dancer scraped along the rock bottom. They tumbled over and over again. Lifted back up into the surge of the wave, they collided with a rock wall. Another surge of water carried them up and over the wall. Down they fell on the other side, scraping along the sandy bottom. Blown like tumbleweed, a pair of orphaned sea urchins rolled past.

Through the lacy gills, Siona saw hope. "There!" she cried. "To the left! There's a burrow!"

Dancer rolled to the left and dropped into a long-vacated U-shaped fossil burrow, the engineering efforts of some wormish creature 20.8 million years earlier, a creature unnamed and unknown, except for the path it cut, marking the border in time between the Ediacaran and Cambrian periods. It was a burrow with a big long name—*Treptichnus pedum*. In trepidation, Siona and her friends huddled. Above the burrow, the water roared.

*   *   *

"**D**inner is ready," called Siona's father from the kitchen.

"Oh no!" cried Siona the human, "We can't stop now! They just fell into a burrow!"

"What?" said Siona's father, stepping from the kitchen with bright yellow oven mitts on his hands. "But it's your favorite. It's my famous spinach lasagna."

"Can we please finish the story after dinner?" Siona asked her mother. "I have to know what happens next."

"Of course," replied her mom. "We're getting close to the end."

Siona and her mother headed to the kitchen and to the heady aroma of Siona's father's famous spinach lasagna. Siona accidently kicked the RatTrap game that she and Gracie Alice had set up the previous Friday. The ball fell from the bucket, rolled down the yellow ladder and red twisty ramp, and collided with the pole that held the cage positioned over the blue plastic rat. Down fell the cage, catching the rat. A whole train of events triggered by one little bump. Siona laughed as she walked into the kitchen. Her father lifted his famous spinach lasagna from the oven.

Siona pressed her fingertips into her father's forearm, right above the bright yellow oven mitts.

"Hey, be careful," said her father. "This dish is really hot!"

"But did you feel that?" asked Siona, pressing a finger again against her father's arm, making a tiny dimple.

Her father glanced at Siona's mother, who simply smiled. Siona's father maneuvered the hot dish to the trivets on the dining room table and then took his seat at the head of the table.

"So what's this all about?" he asked. "And yes, I did feel it."

"Do you remember the fireflies from Ohio?" Siona asked her parents.

"Yes, I do," replied her mother.

"It was really hot," said Siona. "We couldn't sleep, and we were all out on the back porch, drinking ice water. And there they were, the fireflies, turning off and on like tiny, flying flashlights above the lawn. They must have that special light-making widget in them like the dinoflagellates in the story."

"That's right," said Siona's mother.

"And what does this have to do with poking me in the arm?" asked Siona's father.

"It's like the RatTrap game," said Siona. "First, you bump the bucket, and the ball falls, making a whole bunch of other things happen until the cage falls down on the rat."

"What?" asked Siona's father. Siona's mother laughed.

"It's like when Siona the Sea Squirt beat her tail in the water, making bubbles. And the bubbles outside the dinoflagellates banged against them, causing a whole chain of events inside the cells so that they released millions and millions of bits of light. It's like when I touch your arm—probably all sorts of things happen on the inside so you can feel what happens on the outside."

"Oh, that makes sense," said Siona's father, serving his daughter a square of his famous lasagna. "I get it now. You're talking about signal transduction cascades. Pretty cool stuff."

With the meal served, Siona and her mother thanked Siona's father. They ate their meal together, with Siona making "yummy" noises with nearly every bite. "If I were a sea hare, this would be like eating the best red algae ever!"

Siona's father shook his head, and Siona's mother laughed again. When they finished dinner, Siona cleared the table, and her mother did the dishes. Siona's father retired to his study to contemplate moth metamorphosis or the opposite of that. A month ago, he had discovered a mutant moth, a white-lined sphinx that fed solely on the willow weed, its mutation such that it never became a moth but crept into adulthood while still a caterpillar.

Siona picked up a moist dish rag and added some soap. "So how did it all start?" she asked, wiping the table clean.

"What do you mean?" asked her mother.

"The whole thing—the earth, the sun, our galaxy, the universe, the start of time?"

"Oh, that," said her mother, drying a plate. "We can almost see back to the very beginning, some 13.82 billion years ago with the tools and calculations we have, back to less than one billionth of a second after the expansion of the known universe." She picked up another plate, drying it with circular sweeping movements of the dish towel. "It's the big bang theory," she continued, "perhaps a result of a single accidental occurrence of instability in a compressed dot of mass and energy, and *bang!* The universe expanded into the heavens."

"What made that dot of mass? Where did it come from?" asked Siona.

"We don't know yet. According to our current models, it was just there," said Siona's mother.

"So it was there before the beginning of time?" asked Siona, hanging the dish rag over the faucet. "Gracie Alice's father says that God existed before the beginning of time too. So is God like mass?"

Siona's mother stopped drying the dishes. "I don't know," she said. "That's not a question I can answer. Science addresses the physical world, the natural world. I don't have a clue how to design an experiment to test the nature or existence of God. But if I could, it would be some dose-response curve." She laughed, brushing Siona's hair back over her shoulders. "Those are some big questions you are asking, but how about continuing our story. Go take a seat on the rocking chair. I'm almost done with the dishes, and I'll be right there."

Siona walked over to the rocking chair and waited for her mother. "You know," Siona called to her mother, "maybe the next time when you need to collect samples at the beach, I can help."

10

A New Home

HEARTBEATS. SIONA COULD HEAR THEM pounding deep in the fossil burrow, wrapped up so tightly together they might as well have been one animal. The five hearts of each worm. The racing heart of the hare. The beat of the dancer. Bernie's heart, squeezing so close she could feel it in her own tail. The constant flow through the star, like the whoosh of water through microscopic canals. Had they made it to a new home? In the calculations of the odds, were they on the right side of the equation?

Siona, wrapped in the lacy gills, heard the heartbeat of the dancer stutter. She felt the dancer shudder and the tension in the frills relax. Dancer unfurled the roll that was her body. Siona wiggled her tail, leaving the lacy gills for freedom. The others followed, tumbling from the dancer to the bottom of the U-shaped chamber of the ancient burrow. Dancer fluttered.

Siona turned to thank the dancer and cried out in a long wail of mourning when she saw what remained. One long cut coursed its way across the colors of the dancer. It was deep and jagged. Scrapes and bruises wreaked havoc on the carpet-like body. Siona cried out to Bernie as she tried to fill the wound with her remaining blue nanoscale whiskers and cellulose blend. Bernie had no more to give.

"Dancer, Dancer!" Siona cried. "I don't think I can fix you!" And she pressed her head into the dancer's frills as they leached their bold colors. "Thank you, Dancer. Thank you for everything." She swam to where she could hear the dancer's heartbeat and touched her head right there. "Thank you for my life," Siona whispered.

Dancer moved feebly, her frills torn. The others gathered around. Harold stroked Dancer's back with his rhinophores; the worms caressed her with their paddles; Sydney wrapped two arms gently around the weakening creature. Bernie touched her softly. The dancer smiled.

The tattered frills fluttered in the water. Siona's gaze met that of the dancer. The dancer beckoned, and Siona followed her out of the burrow. The monstrous waves from the tsunami and wind had ended; only a long, slow flow crept inland across the pool. Dancer gazed in the direction of the open ocean.

In the center of the pool, a tablet-like rock rose from the sandy bottom, an open book waiting for the story to begin. Dancer led Siona and Bernie to this rock. A small wall rose on the upper left-hand corner of the tablet-like rock. Dancer guided Siona and Bernie behind the small wall. With great relief, Bernie seized the moment.

"What a lovely rock!" cried Bernie. He settled head down on the rock, singing happily. "Find a rock, a good strong rock on which to dock!"

Siona gazed at the black rock below. It glinted with mica and quartz. A swath of obsidian ran down the spine. And she was there too; her reflection stared back from the dark mirror of the rock, her tail waving. A group of rotifers twirled past, crying hello and goodbye as they changed from balls to long bats. The tip of Siona's tail tingled. When she looked up from the rock, she saw her friends had formed a circle around her.

"If it had not been for you, Siona," Kate said softly, "Reilly never would have been in the nursery of the white squirts. He would not have been there to rescue them. All of them would have been lost. They never would have had a chance. And I ... I ... never would have met such a humble and gallant worm." Kate swallowed, glancing down, as Reilly touched one of her paddles with his.

"There are hundreds of us hares," said Harold. "But you made me feel like I was one in a trillion. I'd never sung even one note before I met you, and I don't think I ever would have. You helped me appreciate my ink and my rhinophores. You made me feel special."

"I felt like a misfit. My hydraulic systems were busted," Sydney said with a sigh. "When I lost my arm, I thought that I would never be whole again." He reached out with one arm and touched Siona with a single tiny foot. "But you showed me that even a four-armed star could live again."

"And I would never have had a chance to ride that portal!" cried Bernie. "That was epic!" He paused and then said, "I'm an orange-tainted squirt, and you accepted me for who I am." Bernie touched Siona's tail with his. "And … and you are the most beautiful squirt I ever have seen. I'd swim into any ocean, just to be with you!"

The flow of the ocean ebbed, its advance on the land halted. It started to reverse course, flowing back to the ocean from which it had come.

"Thank you," Siona whispered. "I thank all of you for all that you have done. I feel like we are connected. You're my family!" Her tail shook. She saw Reilly glance at her wavering tail.

"Siona, let's swim an upside-down, inside-out circle one more time together," said the worm.

Siona nodded, her tail tingling. She swam alongside the worm as they gained speed. Reilly called "Now," and up they lifted. Swimming up and backward and upside down and side by side, they managed a near-perfect circle. That is, the circle Siona made was perfect, and she ended up right where she had started. Reilly, on the other hand, twisted a bit out of control at the top of the circle. He spiraled downward, barely missing the rock, and corkscrewed his way to his fifth segment in the sandy bottom. He wrestled himself free from the sand and grit, casting debris every which way. When he tried to speak, he sputtered sand. The animals laughed. Bernie laughed so hard he almost broke free from the rock to which he had just glued his head.

Siona laughed, and then she cried, still wrestling with mixed emotions and mixed genes, the expressive bits of DNA from her complex parentage. "That was my last one, wasn't it? I'm right back where I started. Just like swimming an inside-out, upside-down circle! I am going to grow up with my head stuck to a rock forever and ever, aren't I?" Siona opened her eyes wide, and she smiled. "Because this is who I am. I am a squirt. Isn't that right? I'm a squirt." She swept her tail before her eyes and kissed her jewel goodbye. The tingling in her tail traveled down her back to the tip of her head, her transition to adulthood in progress.

"That's right," cried Bernie. "You are one beautiful, crazy squirt, and we can be crazy squirts together." Bernie pointed at the rock with his tail. "And this rock is the most perfect rock of all. This rock rocks! Come on; stick your head right by mine, and we can be best friends forever! Why don't you try to sing the rock song now?"

Siona started to hum, and then she sang a few notes.

"You can do it!" cried Bernie. "You can sing the song! Give it another try!"

Siona, with her eyes wide open in disbelief, sang. She was off-key, and her words were different. But at last Siona could sing.

> My time has come to find a rock,
> The one that I have left unsought.
> Gone my lovely tail will be
> To give to a future I cannot see.

Overhead, Dancer stumbled (if one can do such a thing in water). She dropped roughly to the rock. She tried to swim upward again, but the effort was too great. The animals surrounded her. She fluttered weakly before them, her colors gone.

"What should we do? Dancer, how can we help?" asked Kate.

Dancer looked overhead. The water that had rushed onto the land was now making its exit, forging its way back to the open sea. Dancer followed the flow of the water with her eyes. Reilly whispered to Sydney and Harold. Harold began to play a song that rose from his rhinophores, like a tune played by bagpipes. The song, a dirge to say goodbye, resounded in the newfound tide pool. Sydney armed his way under the weakening body of the dancer.

Reilly paddled next to Siona, his gaze on the fluttering, lovely Spanish dancer. "Are you ready?" he asked the fluttering creature. Reilly turned to Siona. "Even Dancer wants her last chance to swim out there." He motioned back to the sea. "She wants to swim back to her beginnings."

Dancer nodded as Sydney readied his hydraulics to send the dancer out to sea. Under the body of the dancer, the star's tube feet extended, exploding. Dancer was launched high into the water overhead, where she spun, her frills waving. Seized by the current, she was carried back home to the open ocean.

With Bernie beside her, Siona started to glue her head to the rock. It was not completely unpleasant, though it did take Siona longer than the average squirt to make the transition to her new sedentary lifestyle, such was the mix of her genes. Bernie also transitioned to his squirt form, boasting a set of orange racing stripes on his bright white tunic. In time, Siona's head was anchored to the rock, and she donned a dark blue translucent tunic of cellulose. A little piece of her tail remained between her siphons. Siona was enthralled by the wonders of her new siphons. She squirted at everything, including Bernie, and of course Bernie could not help but squirt her in return.

Her mother had been right. The sea and gentle currents that flowed into the newfound tide pool brought them all the food they needed. And the rays of the sun that penetrated the shallow waters brought them warmth and brilliance—and something else. So bright was the sun over Bernie and Siona that they were blessed. Ultraviolet light tweaked a nucleotide here and nucleotide there in the DNA of the two sea squirts, creating a few changes that Siona, as a free-swimming larva, had desperately sought. But most changes take time—generations of time.

Reilly, Kate, Harold, and Sydney, still mobile and able, kept Siona and Bernie up-to-date with current events. As time went by, Reilly and Kate had offspring of their own. The new worms were a motley assortment of red and yellow. Reilly said they were yellow with red spots, but Kate insisted they were red with yellow spots. Harold stumbled upon another of his kind, who shared his deep love for red algae. They sang happy songs together while munching on clumps of algae. Sydney's fifth arm grew back, and he found happiness with a delicate white star, who was much stronger than her appearance let on. She had such fine control of her hydraulics that she could spin from arm tip to arm tip, while Sydney looked on with admiration. "She is such a star!" he would say with a sigh, his feet wiggling in all five of his arms.

And Siona grew up. She released her eggs, tiny globes, each with a message for the future. Both Siona and Bernie cried when the eggs hatched. They held each other tight with their siphons, amazed by the wonder of the new lives they had created.

There were nearly a thousand of the new little larvae. Some of the sea squirt larvae were white, some blue, some with orange racing stripes like Bernie, and others with long tails like Siona. But all of them loved to swim. They dashed about overhead calling to their parents, "Look at me! Look at me do a loop the loop now." They swam circles around Bernie and Siona. They swam circles around each other. They raced across the pool, swimming upside down. They swam upside-down, inside-out circles with Reilly (though for Reilly, this was still a challenge, and he often corkscrewed deep into the sandy bottom up, to his fourth or fifth segments).

The young sea squirt larvae were great swimmers. But to Bernie's dismay, they were shoddy singers. Hardly any of them knew the sea squirt larvae song that had been passed down for so many generations.

Bernie tried to instruct his children and sang the song for them. "Listen, you guys, the song goes this way," Bernie declared to the dubious larvae.

> Find a rock,
> Find a rock,
> Find a rock on which to dock.
> Time is ticking in your clock.

Siona was no help in teaching her children how to sing. Instead, she shook her siphons like pom-poms. "Swim faster! Swim faster! While you have a tail, swim faster!"

"No, no," said Bernie, holding his head with his siphons.

Siona laughed. "Oh, Bernie, just think what you and I did when we were larvae." And she used her left siphon like a garden hose on a hot summer day, squirting at the children. Scores of rotifers joined in, sliding down the current from Siona's siphon as if on a water slide. The larvae leaped, swimming into the current with peals of laughter that echoed from the rocks. One daughter swam straight into the current, her tail so long it made waves of its own, her bright racing stripes glinting in the sun. She swam right past Siona and Bernie and kept on going.

"Go! Go!" Siona encouraged her. She laughed, remembering when she too had a tail. Long ago she had calculated the odds of growing up. And here she was, stuck to a rock with larvae of her own. Siona smiled. Against the odds and because of the odds, she and her family of friends had survived. As Kate had so adroitly written in the sand, in the calculation of risk, there is also the possibility of success. They had found a new home, a new tide pool, a theater for all that would happen next in their lives.

Rap! Rap! Poke. Bernie poked Siona with a siphon. "Look," he said. "Look there. I hope those squirts will grow up and find a rock soon."

He pointed with his other siphon to a group of their young larvae. With their long tails, they tickled a dozen rotifers. The rotifers sprang from balls to bats and shrunk from bats to balls.

Siona gave Bernie a hug with her two blue siphons. "Don't worry, Bernie. They will grow up. It will happen. It even happened to us."

And Bernie, stuck to a rock by his head, gazed adoringly at Siona. Siona, glued to the same rock, smiled back. The cries and calls and hoots and shouts of their children rose high above the mighty roar of the ocean.

The end.

* * *

"**W**ait," said Siona, sitting next to her mother on the rocking chair and rubbing her eyes, "Are you sure it's over? Doesn't the story go on?"

Siona's mother laughed. "Yes, Siona, the story does go on."

"Oh," said Siona, "tell me what happens next."

"Well, what happens next is almost a story of its own," said Siona's mother, reaching for her daughter's hands and holding them in hers. "Once upon a time, about 450 million years ago, long before you were born, Siona the Sea Squirt's great-great—many greats—granddaughter did what Siona wanted to do. She kept right on swimming, like the fish she was, and did not ever consider sticking her head to a rock."

"Yippee!" cried Siona. "Siona the Fish did what Siona the Sea Squirt wanted to do! Her wish came true!"

"It did," said her mother.

"And then?" asked Siona.

"One day Siona the Fish's great-great-granddaughter pushed with her tail and her strong lobbed fins to clamber over the rocks at the edge of the water. She lunged into the air and caught a dragonfly resting on a fern at the water's edge in her stout jaws."

"And then? And then? The story cannot end there either! It still has to go on. We never got to what happens two million years ago, or what about 195,000 years ago?"

"Siona's great-great-great—many, many, greats—granddaughter ran from the sea and walked along the beach, picking up seashells in her hands."

"And then what? What happened after that? What happens right now?" asked Siona.

Siona's mother looked at her daughter. "What happens right now is that Siona goes to bed."

"Well, what about tomorrow?" asked Siona. "The story has to continue tomorrow."

"It does. Tomorrow we go to the beach—to a new beach, one that you haven't seen before."

Siona stared across the silver ocean. Her father opened the big umbrella. It was blue with orange tassels that waved in the breeze. Siona placed her towel down under the umbrella and pulled her new backpack from her shoulders. Her mother had given it to her earlier that morning. On its surface, an embroidered blue wave rose, curling over a scallop shell, sand dollar, and sea star. Siona grasped the seahorse zipper tab and opened the main pocket. Turning the backpack upside down, she freed the contents, and they spilled out, escaping to the towel below—her blue bucket and shovel, sunglasses, sunscreen, water bottle, and half a dozen pieces of colored sea glass. She had not brought her book. She shook her backpack. The picture she had drawn the day before of the towering wave slipped out and landed upside down. She turned it over. Shaking her head, she crumpled the paper into a ball and tossed it into her backpack. Next, Siona arranged the sea glass in a line above her towel.

Picking up her shovel, she pushed it into the sand above the sea glass. Her shovel hit something hard. She dug in the sand with her hands to retrieve the object. It was a shell. She held it in her hand and turned it over. She tilted the shell, and a wave of iridescence rolled across the surface. With her finger, she traced the path of the wave. Holding the shell carefully in the palm of her hand, Siona knelt on her towel. She unzipped the little back pocket of her backpack as her mother placed a towel on the sand beside Siona's.

"I really like this shell," said Siona to her mother. And she dropped the little gray shell into her backpack for safekeeping.

Her mother sat down and opened her backpack to show Siona the gauged pipette, test tube rack, and the bag of microcentrifuge tubes. "I brought extra gloves for you," said Siona's mother. "And a black marker so you can help label the tubes, if you like. And this, too, for you to use." She lifted another pipette from her backpack. "I can show you how—if you want to, that is. You don't have to come with me if you don't want to."

Siona reached across her towel and gave her mom a hug. "That is so way cool! I'm going to learn how to use a pipette!" She covered her face in her hands, her laughter squeezing between her fingers. "It's so great to be a nerdy weirdo!"

Her mother smiled in agreement, pointing away from the ocean to the dunes. "And we can go inland to a swampy area in the dunes. You won't have to go anywhere near the sea. Would you like to come with me?"

"Yes, yes!" said Siona, jumping up.

Her mother stood up and gave Siona a hug. She picked up own backpack, checked its contents to make sure that they would have all the tools they needed to collect samples from the microbial mats, zipped it up, and swung it to her shoulders. They walked hand in hand until Siona felt compelled to run circles around her mother as they advanced to the dunes. Her mother stepped over strands of kelp and aged driftwood, while Siona jumped over the same objects at a run. Her mother laughed each time Siona circled. "Run, Siona, run!"

Siona heard hoots and shouts above the cries of gulls. She stopped her orbit around her mother, panting. She blocked the sun with one hand. Down the beach, a group of teenagers tossed a Frisbee. It spiraled from one to the next, spinning orange and white, until Siona realized that it was not a Frisbee at all but a five-pointed sea star.

Her mother stopped when Siona's orbits ceased. "What's wrong?" she asked.

"I need to save that sea star before it is too late!" cried Siona, pointing down the beach. She took off running, her footprints leaving a trail behind.

Her mother stared at the trail of footprints below. She slipped her backpack from her shoulders and dropped it behind a driftwood log. She stood up, brushed her hair back behind her shoulders, and, stepping onto the trail of footprints, ran after her daughter.

When Siona reached the star, it was upside down. It had fallen with a thud after its airborne flight, like an unwanted toy cast aside by a bored child. Its tube feet wiggled. Siona knelt beside the creature. A shadow descended, and she looked up to see her mother standing over her.

"Can we save it?" asked Siona.

"We'll need to get it back to the water right away," said her mother. "Over there"—she pointed to a wall of rocks by the ocean—"there's a tide pool among the rocks. It would be a wonderful new home for this star."

Siona picked up the star and cradled it in her hands.

"I'll take it there, so you don't have to go near the water," said her mother.

"It's okay," said Siona, holding the star and trotting to the rocks. Her mother followed. Watching the timing of the waves, Siona jumped up on the rocks. She was greeted by a vast tide pool. She smiled when she saw other sea stars clinging to the black rock. Her star was sure to find some friends here. She stepped along the edge of the pool, careful to avoid the urchins with their black quills nestled in their rocky lacunae. As she knelt by the water, she startled a ragworm. It slipped under a rock. Siona made a note not to disturb that rock. Above the sea creatures, her reflection smiled back. As Siona slid the sea star down into the water, the reflection of her fingertips reached to touch her fingers. She held the star close to the rock, her hand gripping its rough covering, waiting for the creature to give some sign that it still clung to life. She closed her eyes and waited. She felt it move. She released her hold, and the star remained, a bright spot anchored to the dark rock.

A single salty tear fell from above and splashed onto her bare arm. Siona stood up; the tear cascaded down her arm and joined the water below. Siona reached up to her mother's cheek and wiped away the tear that followed.

"We gave that sea star a chance, didn't we?" asked Siona. "A chance to cast its DNA into the future for millions and millions of years to come."

Her mother nodded, wiping her eyes.

They jumped from the rock down to the soft sand below. Down the beach, Siona's father waved his arms, calling for their attention. Mother and daughter ran together down the beach to join him. He was wearing his new swimming trunks, the ones with neon-orange racing stripes. He bolted into the water, swimming with sure strokes. Between the roll of the waves, he did a handstand, his wet shins and feet rotating clockwise above the water.

Siona laughed. "Look! He's trying to do an underwater circle again," Siona cried as the shins and feet leaned left, splayed apart, leaned right, and then fell with a splash into the water.

Siona put her hands above her eyes and waited. She grinned when she saw her father riding in on the next wave. When the water could carry him no longer, he sprang to his feet, racing from the foam to the beach. He ran to Siona and her mother, shaking his head as he sped past. They jumped from the deluge of the spray.

"You're worse than a puppy!" Siona hollered after her father, who raced down the beach, barking like a puppy in play.

Siona and her mother laughed. Siona felt her mother's hand close around hers.

"We can go together," said Siona, "I'll hold your hand."

"I'd like that," said her mother.

"I think I'm 68 percent grown up now," said Siona, looking at her mother. Her mother's hand squeezed hers. Siona took a tiny step to the sea. The incoming surf covered her feet, sucking out the sand beneath her toes with its retreat back to the sea. She pulled the salt air deep into her lungs, raising her shoulders, her heart pounding. Gripping her mother's hand, Siona took another step forward out onto the wet sand. The next wave surged in greeting, calling with its thunder; the percussion echoed from the dunes. The wave rolled out like a carpet in open invitation. The white foam of the wave formed bracelets around her ankles. Siona looked at her mother with a smile. And the two, mother and daughter, ran jumping into the curl of the waves. Siona returned to the company of the waves. She dove into the sea and swam like a fish.

"Look! Look at me!" she called to her mother. "I'm Siona, and I love to swim!"

Her mother laughed, swimming beside her daughter. The two of them blew bubbles, and they dove under the water. They came up for air, swimming beside a surfer resting on his board. His hair a halo of gold. He gave a nod to Siona and paddled out along the path of the sun as if he owned the place, his dark wetsuit gleaming.

"Let's go back to Dad," said Siona, swimming with sure strokes back to the shore.

Siona rose from the waves, the sea a cape flowing from her hair. Her mother followed, stopping when she reached Siona's father. But Siona continued to run full force down the beach. Her feet sinking into the sand left deep footprints in memory of her passage.

"We made a beautiful baby, didn't we?" said Siona's father.

"I think much more made Siona. It's what we believe," said Siona's mother, her words caught in the crash of the waves and the cries of the gulls.

And Siona, not looking back, continued her headlong run down the beach.

Glossary

Actin is a filamentous, threadlike protein. It is involved in muscle contraction, cell motility, cell shape, and the movement of vesicles and organelles in a cell.

Aerobic refers to using or requiring oxygen for growth.

Algae are unicellular or multicellular organisms that contain chlorophyll to capture light energy like plants. Unlike plants, however, algae do not have true stems, leaves, or roots.

Alpha 1,4 bonds and beta 1,4 bonds are chemical bonds between sugars. These are also called glycosidic bonds or linkages. Sugars are rings of carbon, oxygen, and hydrogen. In the ring, each sugar has a number. In 1,4 bonds, the carbon in position 1 is connected to the carbon in position 4 of the adjoining sugar. The sugars are connected through an oxygen atom. The sugar rings are in a plane. In the alpha 1,4 configuration, the oxygen between the two sugars is below the plane of the sugars. In the beta 1,4 configuration, the oxygen is above the plane of the sugars. With this simple alteration, one can either obtain the digestible starch of a potato or the indigestible cellulose of a sea squirt tunic.

Alzheimer's disease is a progressive neurodegenerative disease that destroys memory and other brain functions. Currently, there is no cure for this disease.

Amoebas are single-celled organisms.

Amino acids are the building blocks of proteins, and in this story, they are the building blocks of widgets.

Ammonites are an extinct group of marine mollusks with curved spiral shells. They are the descendants of bacrites and precursors of cephalopods, such as squids, octopuses, and cuttlefish.

Adenine, thymine, guanine, and cytosine are the building blocks for the genetic information in DNA. They are known as nitrogenous bases.

Anaerobic organisms grow in the absence of oxygen.

Annelid is the phylum of segmented worms, including earthworms and ragworms.

Aristotle was a Greek philosopher and scientist (384–322 BC). He mistakenly classified adult sea squirts as mollusks.

ATP or adenosine trisphosphate is composed of a base (adenine) and a five-carbon sugar with three phosphate groups. ATP stores energy in its bonds between the phosphate groups. When ATP breaks down to ADP (adenosine diphosphate), energy is released to power muscle cells and brain cells, other cell functions, and enzymatic reactions. ATP is biological energy.

ATP synthase is a widget or enzyme that generates ATP, thereby releasing energy.

Bacrites are considered to be the precursors of cephalopods, such as squids and cuttlefish and the extinct ammonites. They boast long, straight shells.

Bioenergetics is the study of the processes by which living organisms generate energy. Biochemists sometimes refer to mitochondria and glycolysis as bioenergetic engines.

Bioluminescent organisms are capable of producing and emitting light (photons). Fireflies, some bacteria, and dinoflagellates are capable of bioluminescence.

Biomineralization is the process that living creatures use to produce or sequester minerals to harden tissues or surfaces. Examples include shells in marine invertebrates and bones in people. Clarissa's shell and the spines of Helamite were produced via biomineralization.

Brachipods are marine invertebrates with two shells. Unlike the shells of mollusks, such as clams, the dorsal (top) and ventral (bottom) shells are not the same size. A typical brachiopod has a stalklike pedicle, or foot, that protrudes from the body through a pedicle valve in one of the shells.

Calcite lenses consist of calcium and carbonate with the chemical formula $CaCO_3$. Though optically transparent, calcite is not the best material for an image-forming visual system and can result in a blurred image. The trilobite had calcite lenses in his mosaic eyes.

Calcium-dependent channels are those that open or close in response to calcium. For example, channels in the cell membrane or in the membranes of intracelluluar reservoirs (i.e., bags inside cells) open when calcium binds to a specific widget or protein. The dinoflagellates used calcium-dependent channels in the activation of luciferase to become bioluminescent.

Carbonaceous is an adjective used to describe an object such as a rock, asteroid, or the scale of an animal that contains carbon. The scales of *Wiwaxia* are carbonaceous.

Cellulose is an abundant, naturally occurring polymer. It is composed of glucose molecules connected to each other via a specific beta 1,4 bond between the sugars, creating a polysaccharide (poly = many, and saccharide = sugar). With the beta 1,4 bond, cellulose cannot be broken apart (digested) except by special enzymes. Cellulose is a key component of plant cell walls and bark. It is used to make paper and other products. It is rarely found in animals; sea squirts are an exception.

Celsius is a temperature scale in which water freezes at zero degrees and boils at one hundred degrees. It is used by scientists and in most parts of the world. Americans use Fahrenheit as their temperature scale.

Centimeter is a unit of measurement. There are one hundred centimeters in a meter.

Channels in biological systems are protein widgets that form pores in the cell membrane and organelles. Ions go through these channels to move from one side of a membrane to another. Ion channels are often used in the propagation of electrical impulses.

Charnia masoni is an Ediacaran fossil shaped like a leaf or frond. Siona the human and her mother see the fossil remains of these creatures in chapter 1.

Chemolithotrophic refers to organisms that obtain energy through the oxidation of inorganic molecules, such as sulfur and other chemicals. These organisms are growing by the black smoker chimneys in chapter 9.

Chitin is similar to cellulose. It is a polysaccharide of a derivative of glucose molecules connected to each other via a beta 1,4 bond. It is found in the exoskeletons of shrimp and insects and in fish scales.

Chordata is the phylum of Chordates.

Chordates are animals that have common characteristics, including a notochord that occurs at some point in the animal's life history. All vertebrates, including humans, are chordates.

Cionagracilens is a made-up word. *Ciona* is the genus name of sea squirts. *Gracilens* is the species name of the extinct presumptive chordate, *Pikaia gracilens*. The names were combined to create a unique hybrid. This word appears in the zoological classification of Siona the Sea Squirt in chapter 3.

Clocks or circadian rhythms drive biological functions at specific times during an approximate twenty-four-hour cycle. In this story, biological clocks triggered the hatching of sea squirt larvae.

Codons are the genetic code in the DNA sequence. Rather than using snail shells of different colors, the four basic units of a codon are the four bases of DNA—adenine (A), thymine (T), guanine (G), and cytosine (C). Any three of these in a specific sequence can be used to generate a codon. The three DNA bases or "triplets" are first transcribed to an RNA molecule. Instead of thymine, the RNA molecules contain uracil (U). The RNA codon is then translated to a specific amino acid in the protein sequence. Mutations of this code can alter protein function and may lead to new traits or to disease. For example, in sickle cell anemia there is a mutation in the DNA sequence that codes for the twentieth amino acid in one of the proteins that makes hemoglobin. The correct codon is GAG, which codes for glutamic acid, and the mutated codon is GUG, which codes for valine.

Concentration gradients result when there is a higher concentration of a particle or molecule in one cellular compartment as compared to another. This represents potential energy, as molecules will move down their concentration gradients to establish equilibrium.

Coprolite is fossilized feces or dung.

Cryogenic test tube racks maintain samples at cold temperatures.

Cytoplasm is the goo and stuff inside a cell, excluding the organelles and nucleus.

Cytoskeletal proteins, such as microtubules, actin, and myosin, play a role in cell shape, motility, and cell division. *Cyto* refers to *cell*.

Depolymerization occurs when subunits are no longer connected together in a filament, such as when tubulin monomers depolymerize from microtubules.

Dermis is the layer in skin below the epidermis.

Diatoms are mostly unicellular algae that can group together to form colonies. Their cell walls are made of silica, a component of glass.

Dickinsonia costata is an extinct ovoid organism from the Ediacaran period characterized by radial segments. Siona and her mother see the fossil remains of this creature as they walk on the beach. It is also in the picture that Siona draws in chapter 1.

Diurnal animals are awake and active during the day.

DNA is the acronym for deoxyribonucleic acid and is the hereditary material that passes from one generation to the next. DNA is composed of the bases adenine, thymine, guanine, and cytosine, and a sugar-phosphate backbone. DNA is often described as the "blueprint" or the "recipe" for an organism. DNA is "expressed" (see Gene Expression, below) into proteins at a given time in a given location. In this story, DNA expression was expressed as a song or musical score.

Dorsal is the top surface of an animal or plant.

Dose-response curves measure a biological response to a specific amount or concentration of a drug or other stressor.

Echinoderm is a phylum that consists of animals with radial symmetry, such as sea urchins and sea stars.

Electrochemiluminescent (ECL) tags release light when electrically stimulated in the presence of certain chemistries. Measuring biomarkers is one application of ECL.

Electron microscopes use a beam of accelerated electrons instead of light to illuminate samples. This enables resolution and imaging of much smaller cellular structures than those imaged with traditional light microscopes.

Electrochemical gradients are gradients of charged particles or ions. For example, protons (H^+) can generate electrochemical gradients. A gradient is established when there are more particles or charges on one side of a membrane as compared to the other side. Electrochemical gradients are used in energy metabolism and in excitable cells, such as brain and muscle cells.

Electron transport chain is a series of proteins located in the mitochondrial inner membrane. Electrons, generated in the mitochondrial matrix from the tricarboxylic acid cycle, are transported along this chain from electron donors to electron acceptors. Ultimately, they reach the final electron acceptor, oxygen. The pumping of protons from the mitochondrial matrix is coupled to the flow of electrons down the electron transport chain to create an electrochemical gradient that is ultimately used to power the production of ATP.

Epidermis is the top layer of skin over the dermis.

Exoskeleton is a hardened covering of an animal used for protection and support. *Exo* stands for *outer*. This is in contrast to the endoskeletons of vertebrates, including people, where *endo* means *inside*. Insects and animals with shells, such as clams, have exoskeletons.

FADH$_2$ is the acronym for flavin adenine dinucleotide, one of the major electron carriers in the oxidation of fuel molecules. FADH$_2$ carries electrons to the electron transport chain in mitochondria to make ATP.

Fatty acids are an energy source for mitochondria. Fatty acids are "burned" to generate ATP. They are also key components in cell membranes.

Flagella are whiplike structures made of microtubules. Flagella are used for locomotion or to move fluids over the cell surface or tissue. The sponges and Volvox colonies in this story have gigantic flagella because this is a work of fiction.

Genes are the regions of DNA that are translated into proteins.

Gene expression is a term used to highlight where, when, and how much of a gene is translated into protein. Gene expression can follow temporal and spatial rules, depending on the organism. For example, a gene might be expressed only at a certain time (temporal) in the tail of an organism (spatial). In this story, when the sea squirts sing their songs about finding a rock, they do so because of an underlying pattern of gene expression. Different squirts from different genetic backgrounds sing different songs. It takes Siona a long time to find the words to the song because of her unique genetic makeup. Her words are very different, and she sings out of key.

Glycolysis is one of two basic bioenergetic processes used to generate ATP or energy for cells. Glycolysis takes place in the cytoplasm of cells and burns sugar to generate energy, much like humans burn coal for the same purpose.

Glycolytic relates to glycolysis.

Green fluorescent protein (GFP) was first discovered in jellyfish. It is a protein made of 238 amino acids. When exposed to blue or ultraviolet light, this protein becomes "excited" and emits green light. GFP was one of the first proteins to become a "reporter" molecule and used by research scientists to measure gene expression.

Hallucigenia sparsa is an extinct marine invertebrate from the Cambrian period. It was given its unusual name because it looks like the product of a wild hallucination.

Histidine kinases are proteins involved in signaling to convey external environmental stimuli internally into cells. They are found in bacteria and other organisms.

Horizontal gene transfer is the lateral movement of genetic material from one organism to another. This contrasts with the vertical transfer of genetic material from parents to offspring through reproduction. In the story, Siona's creation is a result of an accidental horizontal gene transfer event when her egg runs into Propikaia.

Hydrogen ions are hydrogen atoms that have lost their electrons and are designated as H^+. Hydrogen is both the most abundant and smallest of the elements in the universe. In biological systems, H^+ plays a role in signal transduction cascades and in intracellular acidification. In energy metabolism, H^+ plays a role in generating electrochemical gradients.

Hyoliths are extinct marine invertebrates that had cone-like bodies with two skinny lateral "arms."

Hypobranchial glands are found in some mollusks and play a role in mucus secretions, including chemicals that produce dyes, such as Tyrian purple.

Hypotheses are guesses.

Intercellular denotes functions between cells.

Integration is a mathematical expression used to calculate the area under a curve.

Intracellular denotes functions that take place inside a single cell.

Invertebrates are animals that do not have backbones or vertebral columns. These include clams, sea stars, sponges, earthworms, and jellyfish.

Lacunae are cavities or depressions, primarily in bone and cartilage.

Lobopods (gilled) were Cambrian animals that were worm- or arthropod-like.

Luciferase is an enzyme of bioluminescent organisms, such as fireflies and dinoflagellates. In the presence of oxygen, ATP, and its substrate luciferin, the enzyme luciferase catalyzes the production of the high-energy but unstable oxyluciferin. When oxyluciferin "relaxes" to the ground, or lowest energy state, photons are released.

Magma is molten rock beneath the surface of the planet. When magma escapes the earth's crust it becomes lava.

Mechanoreceptors are sensory receptors that respond to mechanical deformations such as touch.

Metamorphosis is the change in form during development, such as the caterpillar becoming the butterfly or the free-swimming sea squirt larva becoming a sedentary bag-like creature.

Microbes are microorganisms, such as bacteria.

Microbial mats are sheets of microbes layered one on top of the other. They are made primarily from bacteria and archaea. Archaea are similar to bacteria but differ in the composition of their cell walls. Archaea typically live in extreme habitats such as hot springs or deep-sea hydrothermal vents.

Microns are a unit of length. One micron is one millionth of a meter.

Microcentrifuge tubes are commonly used in the lab to collect, dilute, and centrifuge samples. They usually have a snap cap.

Microtubules are located inside cells and are cytoskeleton proteins made of tubulin subunits. They elongate by adding tubulin subunits (polymerization), and they shrink by releasing tubulin subunits (depolymerization). Microtubules play key roles in cell division, intracellular transport, and cell motility and shape. Microtubules are key structural proteins in flagella and cilia, as well as in the pseudopodia of radiolarians.

Mitochondria are organelles that serve as one of the two bioenergetic engines in cells to generate energy. Mitochondria have their own DNA and also play key roles in intracellular signaling. They have been implicated in the onset of grave human diseases, such as Parkinson's and Alzheimer's. It is hypothesized that they were once free-living microbes; over a billion years ago they were engulfed by larger microbes, ultimately becoming organelles.

Model organisms are life-forms that have been extensively studied. They are generally easy to maintain and reproduce quickly. Some commonly used model organisms are drosophila (fruit flies), *Mus musculus* (mice), *Arabidopsis thaliana* (weeds), *Caenorhabditis elegans* (worms), and *Aplysia californica* (sea hares or sea slugs). *Aplysia* have been used as model organisms of learning and memory, and sea squirts have been used as model organisms for whole genome analysis (the analysis of all the genes and genetic material in a single organism).

Mother of pearl or **nacre** is the iridescent surface of some mollusk shells. It is a composite material of inorganic and organic constituents. The inorganic portion can be arranged in stacks, like hexagonal tiles of aragonite (a form of calcium carbonate). These tiles are stuck together by the grout of the biological material, which may be similar to chitin or silklike proteins.

Mollusks are soft-bodied invertebrates lacking backbones. They are part of the diverse phylum of Mollusca and include animals such as clams, snails, squids, and slugs. A key attribute of this phylum is the dorsal structure known as the mantle. In shelled mollusks, the mantle contains specialized cells that secrete the materials to make shells.

Mouflon are wild sheep and are thought to be one of the two ancestors of domestic sheep.

Mutations in DNA are defined by how they alter the DNA sequence. There are point mutations that alter only one base, such as swapping an adenine for a guanine. There are deletions that remove bases and insertions that add bases. Whole hunks of DNA can be lost during replication and viral DNA can be inserted.

Myosin is a cytoskeletal protein and, along with actin, plays a starring role in muscle contraction and cell motility.

Nacre (see mother of pearl).

NADH/H⁺ is the acronym for nicotinamide adenine dinucleotide, one of the major electron carriers in the oxidation of fuel molecules. NADH/H⁺ carries electrons to the electron transport chain in mitochondria to make ATP.

Nanometers are units of length. A nanometer is one-billionth of a meter.

Nanoscale whiskers are tiny structures from tunicates (sea squirts) that are reported to align muscle fibers and may support wound healing.

Negatively phototactic is to move away from the light. Sea squirt larvae are negatively phototactic. This makes good sense, as they have to move away from the light and swim to where it is darker to find a good rock. The sea squirt larvae in this story play games to practice negative phototaxis in chapter 3.

Neotenous is an adjective describing the retention of juvenile characteristics in the adult. **Neoteny** could be applied to a frog that became reproductive while still a tadpole or to a moth that became reproductive while still a caterpillar. Walter Garstang, in his posthumously published work (1951), hypothesized that vertebrates are the descendants of sea squirts that never grew up. (See Richard Dawkins, *The Ancestor's Tale: A Pilgrimage to the Dawn of Evolution*. New York: Houghton Mifflin Company, 2005, 367–371). *Siona's Tale* was modeled after this hypothesis.

Neurons are nerve cells that conduct electrical impulses in the brain and in the peripheral (anything in the body outside of the brain) nervous system.

Neohexabranchidae is a made-up family name for a Cambrian Spanish dancer. The prefix *neo* denotes new. This is what Siona's mother writes as a zoological classification in chapter 3.

Notochordus is made up and a play on the word *notochord*. A notochord is a feature of all chordates. A notochord is a rodlike cartilaginous structure that gives way to form the backbone in all vertebrates. Sea squirts have a notochord during their larval stage. In the story, Propikaia had the long name of *Primogenitus notochordus-neotenous*.

Nocturnal animals are awake and active at night.

Nucleotides are the nitrogenous bases (**adenine, thymine, guanine, and cytosine**) along with a sugar group and one or more phosphate groups. Together, these bases, along with the sugar and phosphate backbone, make DNA.

A nudibranch is sluglike marine mollusk, including the colorful Spanish dancer.

Ocelli are "little eyes." Ocelli are the simple eyes of invertebrates that contain photoreceptors, pigments, and other neuronal cells.

Odontogriphus omalus is an oval-shaped creature from the Cambrian period, shaped like a miniature running track. Could it be a descendent of *Dickinsonia costata*?

Olfactory systems are those designed to detect scents or odor molecules.

The Onega Peninsula protrudes into the White Sea between Onega Bay and Dvina Bay in Arkhangelsk Oblast, Russia. Fossils from the Ediacaran period have been found on the Onega Peninsula.

Opabina reglis is an arthropod creature from the Cambrian period that boasts a proboscis and stalked eyes.

Optical fibers are thin fibers made of silica glass or plastic and are used to transmit light.

Order of magnitude is an increase or decrease by a factor of ten. An increase of six orders of magnitude would be an increase of one million.

Organelle means little organ. Organelles are specialized structures inside cells that form compartments for specific functions. Organelles include the nucleus, vacuoles, mitochondria, lysosomes, endoplasmic reticulum, and the golgi apparatus.

Palladium-catalyzed coupling is a process in chemistry that employs palladium as a catalyst to generate new chemical compounds. Three researchers were awarded the 2010 Nobel Prize in Chemistry for their work on palladium-catalyzed cross-coupling. Their methods were used to synthesize discodermolide, a sponge protein shown to have anticancer activity.

Paraformaldehyde is a fixative used to preserve biological samples for analysis via microscopy.

Parapodia are the frills or undulating fins of nudibranches and other mollusks.

Peristaltic hearts pump blood by muscle contraction, much like squeezing a tube of toothpaste.

Petroglyphs are carvings in rocks. Typically, they were created by prehistoric peoples.

Phlegm is that gunky stuff that one can cough up. It is generated by mucous secretions in respiratory passages.

Phosphate rocks are naturally occurring geological formations. They leach the element phosphorous into the environment, which is a known fertilizer. Some theories suggest that high levels of phosphorous and/or phosphates (molecules containing phosphorous) helped trigger the Cambrian explosion.

Photons are the elements of light and exist as both particles and waves. Photons are generated by the sun, stars, and creatures capable of bioluminescence.

Photoreceptors are specialized sensory cells that respond to light stimulation. Specialized proteins in photoreceptors absorb photons, triggering a cascade of biochemical events that generate changes in the electrical signals of the photoreceptors. Different classes or types of photoreceptors are tuned to the absorption of light at particular wavelengths. With multiple classes of photoreceptors, organisms can see in color. For example, humans have three different cone photoreceptors known as blue, green, and red cone photoreceptors. The blue cones, also called S cones (S for short), respond maximally to light at 420 nanometers (nm). The green cones or M (medium) cones respond maximally to light at 530 nm. The red or L (long) cones respond maximally to light at 560 nm. Rod photoreceptors that are employed for night vision respond maximally to light at approximately 500 nm.

Phototransduction is the first step in light detection and vision. It is the series of processes that signal light stimulation, or photon absorption, to the electrical outputs of the photoreceptors.

Phylum is a category into which scientists group living organisms by common features and characteristics. Phylum is a category under "kingdom" and precedes "class" in the current classification system.

Pipettes are laboratory tools that allow researchers to transfer small volumes, such as milliliters or microliters. Pipette can also be a verb, as when a researcher pipettes a sample into a microcentrifuge tube.

Polymerizing molecules undergo elongation as monomeric subunits are added, one on top of the other, to create a polymer.

Polymers are a series of monomers or similar groups connected via chemical bonds to each other. Cellulose and starch are polymers of sugars. DNA is a polymer of nucleotides. Plastics are polymers.

Polysaccharides are polymers of sugars. The term *poly* means many and saccharides are sugars or carbohydrates. Cellulose is a polysaccharide.

Positively phototactic is to move toward the light. Siona the human saves herself from drowning when she becomes positively phototactic.

Preasteriidae is a made-up word using *pre* to mean *before*. Asteriidae designates a class of enchinoderms known as sea stars. *Aster* means *star*. This term is in the classification of the star in chapter 3.

Preenterogona is a made-up word using *pre* to mean *before*. Enterogona is an order of tunicates, such as sea squirts. Siona the human's mother uses this term in the classification of Siona the Sea Squirt in chapter 3.

Priapulid worms or penis worms live in marine environments. Priapulid-like worms were thought to have lived during the Cambrian period and are named after Priapus, a Greek god with a distinct penis.

Primoforcipulatida is a made-up word using *primo* as *first*. Forcipulatida is an order of sea stars.

Primogenitus is a Latin word for first-born.

Proboscis is a long nose of an animal, such as an elephant's trunk. It is also a tubular sucking apparatus in some worms.

Propikaia is a play on the name of a Cambrian chordate called *Pikaia gracilens*.

Propikaicionidae is a made-up word to highlight a hybrid between an early pikaia, a Cambrian chordate, and a sea squirt. *Cionidae* is a family classification of sea squirts. Siona the human's mother uses this term in the zoological classification of Siona the Sea Squirt in chapter 3.

Proteases are enzyme widget proteins that act like little molecular scissors to cut other proteins into peptides or amino acids.

Protoascidiacea is a made-up word using *proto* as *first*, with the class name of *ascidiacea* for a sea squirt. Siona the human's mother uses this term in the zoological classification of Siona the Sea Squirt in chapter 3.

Protonudibranchia is a made-up word using *proto* as *first*, with the name of *nudibranchia* for an early Spanish dancer. Siona the human's mother uses this term in the zoological classification of the Spanish dancer in chapter 3.

Protons are positively charged hydrogen ions. These ions are used for a variety of functions in cells, including intracellular communication, enzyme activation, and in the creation of electrochemical gradients that play a role in energy generation.

Protozoa are unicellular eukaryotic organisms.

Pseudopodia are temporary extensions from amoeboid cells that are used in feeding and movement.

Radiolarians are aquatic, unicellular creatures and are thought to have existed for over six hundred million years. They are graced with elaborate skeletons of silica.

Redox boundaries in marine environments mark the transition between the presence (oxic) and absence (anoxic) of oxygen and play a role in the metabolic strategies of organisms living under these different conditions.

Rhinophores are specialized chemoreceptor or olfactory (scent) sensory organs found in many marine organisms.

Rubisco (RuBisCo, or D-ribulose 1,5-Bisphosphate carboxylase/oxygenase) is one of the most abundant enzymes on our planet. It is found in plants, trees, and other photosynthetic organisms and plays a key role in carbon dioxide fixation, effectively turning plants and trees into CO_2 sinks. The enzyme modifies CO_2 to generate energy-rich sugars.

Scintillons are organelles in dinoflagellates that harbor the bioluminescence machinery—the luciferase enzyme, its substrate luciferin, and, in some species, the luciferin-binding protein. With the acidification of the scintillons, luciferase undergoes a conformational change, binding luciferin. In the species with the luciferin-binding protein, this protein binds luciferin at neutral pH but releases the substrate with acidification. With the acidification of the scintillons, luciferin is converted to the high-energy but unstable oxyluciferin.

Sessile organisms are those that are immobile and cannot move.

Signal transduction cascades are used to communicate events outside a cell to inside a cell. These can be sensory in nature, such as the absorption of light by photoreceptors that leads to membrane hyperpolarization or changes in the electrical output of the photoreceptors. The binding of a hormone to a receptor will also trigger a signal transduction cascade inside a cell.

Silica is used to make glass and is a primary component of sand. It is also a component of the cell walls of diatoms and radiolarians.

Sodium is an element. Sodium ions along with chloride ions are the key players in the salinity, or saltiness, of the sea. There are approximately 10,800 milligrams per liter (mg/L) of sodium in saltwater and approximately 3,220 mg/L sodium in blood.

Starch is a polymer of digestible sugars due to the configuration of the bond between the sugar subunits. Most organisms have the widget proteins necessary to break the alpha 1,4 sugar bonds.

Stem cells are pluripotent, undifferentiated cells capable of becoming different types of cells and tissues, such as muscle, brain, or the cells needed to make a new sea star arm.

Subcellular refers to objects or functions that take place inside cells.

Symbiotic partners are animals that live together for mutual benefit.

Transporters are protein widgets that transport ions, molecules, peptides, amino acids, and even other proteins across cell membranes.

Treptichnus pedum is a burrow from some wormlike creature. This burrow marks the transition from the Ediacaran geological period, spanning from 630 to 542 million years ago, to the Cambrian period, spanning from 542 to 489 million years ago.

Trilobites arc an extinct group of marine arthropods. According to the fossil records, they first arrived approximately 521 million years ago. They are thought to have died off during the Permian extinction about 252 million years ago. Between these two time points, they were an abundant and diverse group of animals.

Tunicates, or the subphylum of Urochordata, are marine invertebrates that have a cellulose-rich tunic. They also possess structures indicative of chordates, such as notochords.

Tunics for marine invertebrates are cellulose-like outer coverings that offer protection. For humans, tunics are loosely fitted tops.

Ultraviolet light is electromagnetic energy with wavelengths of light from 10 to 400 nanometers. It is a mutagen and can damage DNA.

Unicellular organisms are single-celled creatures.

Vacuoles are membrane-bound vesicles in the cytoplasm of cells. They can be digestive organelles in cells, as well as reservoirs to sequester ions, such as protons in dinoflagellates.

Ventral is associated to the underside, or bottom, of an animal or plant.

Vertebrates are animals with backbones, or vertebral columns, and they include cats, dogs, kangaroos, elephants, fish, snakes, and people.

Vitelline membrane is the protective cover of an egg or the yolk in an egg in some species.

Voltage-gated channels are those that are opened or closed, depending on the voltage across the cell membrane.

Volvox is a spherical colony that can be composed of up to fifty thousand unicellular green algae.

Wavelength is the distance between peaks in a wave, whether the wave is from sound, light, or waves in the ocean. Wavelengths of light in the visual spectrum that humans can see is from approximately 400 to 700 nanometers (nm).

Wiwaxia corrugata is an extinct marine invertebrate from the Cambrian period. A key morphological feature was that it was covered with carbonaceous scales.

Zinc is an element and a metal. In biological systems, it is used to strengthen cross-linked fibrous proteins, such as those in ragworm fangs. Zinc also plays a role in catalytic or enzymatic functions, as well as intracellular and intercellular signaling. Cells and organelles have zinc transporters.

Acknowledgments

THIS WORK WOULD NEVER HAVE been completed without my three children. The story started out as two pages and grew as my children grew.

I'm indebted to my husband, Frank, for his love, support, and corrections in enzymology. I am grateful for my sister, Kathy Liepe-Levinson, PhD, for her discussions on the power of stories and the narrative voice. Marty Levinson, PhD, my sister's husband, provided insights and suggestions. My brother, Steve, and his wife, Debbie, influenced specific passages of this book. My neighbor John Griffin asked, over a glass of wine, "Why stop with the fish?" Chris Teuber, my cousin, said, "Just write it, and write it the way you want!" I am extremely grateful to my neighbor Jean Thornton for her corrections on my math and grammar. I am indebted to her patience as she stood at her kitchen door, listening to my ramblings, year after year, on the wonders of marine invertebrates.

I would like to thank the content editors of iUniverse for the flaws they found in the original manuscript and for their numerous suggestions. To Noel Weyrich, my book doctor, I am utterly grateful for his sense of story, structure, and character. Ultimately, I was able to wade into the tide pools with the characters, and they told me what to do next. I would like to provide a very special acknowledgment to my cousin Andreas Teuber, PhD, for his hours and hours of insightful discussion in the early stages of this project. It was Andreas who suggested telling this tale to a child. During our discussions, it was as if Siona sat at the table between us. I also thank Dr. Terry Machen for his insights while a member of my thesis committee and for listening, decades later, to a brief summary of this story. I am grateful to Hans Biebuyck for his words of encouragement. Gunjan Tiwari, I thank you for your comments and for setting me straight so many times.

I cannot thank Cash Briscoe enough for the inspiration and enthusiasm and the drive to rewrite, edit, and do it all over again. I am grateful to Charlene Stone, PhD, with whom I authored a scientific publication years ago when we were both postdocs, for the feedback on the text and the hope she inspired that the story read was finally the one that I had intended to write. I also would like to thank Maureen Powers, PhD, for her feedback and encouragement. I would like to thank the attorney who sat beside me on the plane flying from Seattle to Oakland as I scribbled down the outline for the story in November 2009. When I ran out of paper, he offered me his blank legal pad. I don't know his name.

Of course I would like to thank Charles Darwin and Walter G., and I am deeply indebted to my scientific mentors, Drs. Beth Burnside and David Copenhagen, who even as grown-ups continue to ask questions with zeal and glee. Lastly, I would like to thank my mother for her perpetual encouragement, creativity, and thoughtfulness. Though trained as a painter and artist, she read this story at the age of ninety-one, plowing through the science like a boss. My dad—when I was a teenager, he gave me the book *The Life-Giving Sea* for no reason at all. It's on my bookshelf still.

About the Author

BARBARA A. LIEPE, PHD, IS a sales representative in the life sciences and earned her PhD from the University of California, at Berkeley, studying fish photoreceptors. She has authored several scientific publications. She and her husband, Frank, live in Berkeley, California, and have three children.

About the Illustrator

MADDIE KATHLEEN IS A FREELANCE illustrator specializing in comics and concept art. She graduated in 2017 from the Academy of Art University in San Francisco, and loves designing fantastical worlds and characters

CPSIA information can be obtained
at www.ICGtesting.com
Printed in the USA
FSHW021104221219
65364FS